REAL PEOPLE #4

D0897976

The Real People
Book Four

THE WAY SOUTH

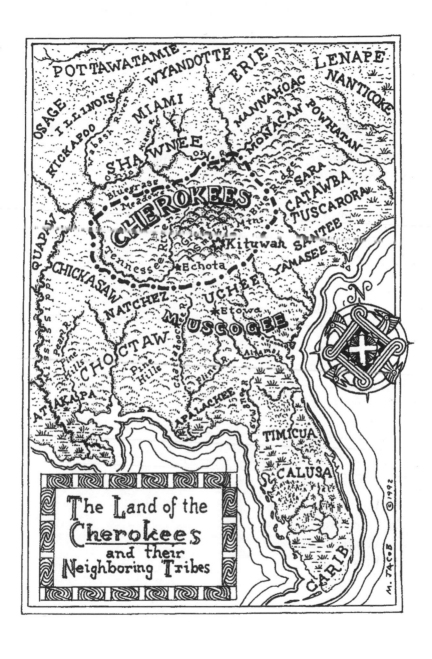

The Land of the
Cherokees
and their
Neighboring Tribes

Also by Robert J. Conley

The Rattlesnake Band and Other Poems
Back to Malachi
The Actor
The Witch of Goingsnake and Other Stories
Wilder and Wilder
Killing Time
Colfax
Quitting Time
The Saga of Henry Starr
Go-Ahead Rider
Ned Christie's War
Strange Company
Border Line
The Long Trail North
Nickajack
Mountain Windsong

The Real People

The Way of the Priests
The Dark Way
The White Path
The Way South

ROBERT J. CONLEY

The Way South

A Double D Western
DOUBLEDAY
New York London Toronto Sydney Auckland

A Double D Western
PUBLISHED BY DOUBLEDAY
a division of Bantam Doubleday Dell Publishing Group, Inc.
1540 Broadway, New York, New York 10036

Double D Western, Doubleday,
and the portrayal of the letters DD
are trademarks of Doubleday, a division of
Bantam Doubleday Dell Publishing Group, Inc.

Library of Congress Cataloging-in-Publication Data

Conley, Robert J.
The way south/Robert J. Conley—1st ed.
    p.   cm.—(A Double D western)
1. Indians—First contact with Europeans—Fiction
2. Cherokee Indians—Fiction.   I. Title.
PS3553.O494W34   1994
813'.54—dc20   93-15770
CIP

ISBN 0-385-42620-8
Copyright © 1994 by Robert J. Conley
All Rights Reserved
Printed in the United States of America
January 1994
First Edition

10 9 8 7 6 5 4 3 2 1

Special thanks to Andrew Barnebey

Historical Note

In 1520 Francisco de Garay took three ships to Florida's northwest coast. He was not the first. The Spanish already knew the land and had named it Florida. Spanish ships had visited Florida's coasts probably since 1510, and the Spaniards had fought with the natives and carried some of them away into slavery. Garay intended to establish a colony in Florida, but he met with "such an unfriendly welcome" that he abandoned his mission.

THE WAY SOUTH

One

"CARRIER," said Long Back, turning over the slab of red rock in his hands, "they say that you're going to go far south on this trip."

"Yes," said Carrier.

"As far as to the country of the Apalachee People?"

"Even farther than that. We plan to trade with the Timucua People, my uncle and I."

"Oh?" said Long Back. "So far? If you go so far south as that, you might see some of the hairy faces we've been hearing about."

Carrier laughed at the thought.

"Do you believe in them?" he asked. "The white-skinned hairy faces who ride on the backs of beasts?"

Long Back was stroking the red slab with the palm of his hand. He shrugged.

"I don't know," he said. "I've never seen one, but others say that they have seen them, I guess."

"Have any of the Real People seen them, do you think?"

"No one from here in Kituwah that I know of, nor anyone else I've talked with claims to have actually seen them. Some Choctaws said that some Apalachees saw them. That's what I heard."

"I heard also that some Chickasaws said that the hairy-faced men had been seen by people to the west," said Carrier. "All of our neighboring peoples say that someone else has seen them."

"Not all of our neighbors. Only those to the south and west of us," said Long Back.

"Yes. Of course," said Carrier. "No one to our east or to our north has reported seeing these strangers. Well then, maybe you're right. Maybe I will meet up with them down in the land of the Timucuas. Maybe I'll even trade with them. If they are real, if these tales we've been hearing are true, they have some strange and wonderful things. It would be interesting to meet these people who come from some unknown place across the water."

"Yes," said Long Back, "if they are people."

Carrier laughed again.

"And if they really exist," he added. "So how do you like the stone?"

"It's a nice one," said Long Back. "I think maybe I can get four pipes out of this one." He gestured toward several finished pipes lying on the ground between him and Carrier. They had been carved from black stone. "Will you take those for it?"

"Yes," said Carrier. "I think that's a good trade."

"I could use some more of this red stone, I think," said Long Back. "If you get some more, come and see me again."

Carrier nodded, but he did not make a verbal reply. He did have some more of the red pipestone, but he wanted to carry it south with him. The red stone came from some place far north, and it was a rare commodity. Long Back's pipes were finely made and traded well wherever Carrier and his uncle Dancing Rabbit took them out of the country of the Real People; therefore, it had been worthwhile to Carrier to trade some of the rare red stone for some of Long Back's finely made pipes. But he did not want to give up all of his precious red stone locally, before the trip had even begun.

As Carrier walked back toward his mother's house along the streets of Kituwah, past the townhouse where most of the men were gathered in the square, lounging about, talking with one another, some watching two others playing at the *gatayusti* game with stone wheel and spear and betting on the outcome, he wondered how late it would be before his uncle got back to town. As soon as Dancing Rabbit brought in the ginseng, they would have everything they wanted, and they would be ready to start the journey. He wondered if they would start in the morning. He hoped so. He was ready to go.

As he passed by the square, some of the men called out greetings, nodded and waved. He responded in kind, smiling. Ordinarily he would be there with them on a day like this in the warm part of the year, the Snake Time, the time they called *Gogi*. But he and his uncle were busy preparing for one of their biggest trading trips of the year. He had no time for leisure.

Dancing Rabbit was far up in the hills. It had taken him at least half the morning to get there, but the ginseng plant was rare and elusive. And to make the gathering of it even more difficult and time-consuming, it was forbidden to take any one of the first six plants one came across. Only the seventh could be taken. But it was worth the effort. It was a valuable trade item.

And Dancing Rabbit, formerly the priest Like-a-Pumpkin, who had been saved from the massacre of the *Ani-Kutani* only by his absence, had a pretty good idea where the plants were to be found. He had already gathered three plants, which meant that he had found twenty-one, but he wanted one more. He had started over counting after he had pulled up his third, and now he had found five. Two more and his task would be done.

He had climbed the hill as far as he could by walking. To get the rest of the way to the top, he would have to climb with arms and legs. It was a steep, rocky way ahead. The roots from the three precious plants were wrapped in a soft skin and tied to the sash around his waist. He reached high over his head and found a hold in some rocks. Then he planted his right foot on another and pulled himself up. In this manner he inched his way to the top.

He dragged himself over the edge and sat down to catch his breath. I'm getting too old for this, he thought. Maybe I should quit after this trip. Maybe along the way this time I should prepare Carrier so that he can go alone in the future.

He had known that the time would have to come sooner or later when his nephew would have to do without him. Well, he thought, still panting from his exertion, maybe this was the time. They would make this one last trip together, and then the younger man would have to take over for himself.

Dancing Rabbit stood and looked around. The air was clear, and the mountains all around were lush and green. He could see all the way to Kituwah down in the valley, and he could see Long Person where his waters ran beside the town.

Then his breath was coming more easily again, and he decided to take up his search. He had but two more plants to find, one to pass by and the next to gather. It shouldn't take long. He was sure that he would find them in this location.

And he did find another one in a short while. The quick success encouraged him, and he went looking for the seventh, the one he could take. Then he would have the four he had come after.

"Where are you hiding?" he sang, improvising, as he poked around the rocks and in the brush. "I have found six others. Now I can have you. Seven, where are you hiding? *Atali-guli*, Mountain Climber, where are you hiding?"

But the seventh was not so easy to locate as had been the sixth. The sun climbed straight overhead to visit her daughter's house in the middle of her journey across the Sky Vault, and, her visit done, she began her western descent.

Then he found it. He almost stepped on it, and it startled him. He dropped down to his knees, the precious plant there before him. He put his hands around it as if to cup it, but he did not touch it. And then he spoke to the mountain.

"Great Man," he said, "I have need of this one small piece of your flesh."

Then he grasped the plant firmly and pulled, drawing out the entire long root from the ground.

"So, Little Man," he said. He took the skin pouch off his sash and opened it up. He placed the plant there beside the other three, and he picked up a small red bead from inside the pouch. He dropped the bead into the hole from which he had pulled the plant, and with the side of his hand, he brushed the dirt back into the hole. He rewrapped the pouch and reattached it to his sash. Then he stood up to leave.

He made his way back to the edge of the mountaintop, the way he had come up. Going down would be more difficult, but he had done it before. He walked to the edge and looked down. He heaved a long sigh. Ah well, he said to himself, it has to be done. He turned around and got down on his hands and knees and started to back his way over the edge.

He felt with his foot for a solid spot on which to stand. When he found one, he started down with the other foot. His hands still grasped sturdy brush on the top. Slowly he let himself down.

He had gone about halfway. His feet were both on solid rock. His hands, about level with his head, gripped large out-croppings of rock. He was getting ready to lower his right foot again when the rock his left hand gripped came loose. His arm swung out, away from the mountainside, and his fist still gripped the rock. He turned his head to look at it, amazed.

"Ah."

He shouted in spite of himself, and he felt his body begin to swing. His right hand still held firm, but his body swung around, out and to the left in a semicircle until he felt his back smash against the mountain. The impact jarred loose his right hand grip, and he pitched forward, head first.

"Aiee!"

He yelled long and loud as he flew through the air, and his body turned over in the air as he fell. When he struck the side of the mountain lower down, his leg hit first. He heard it, and he felt it. He knew that it was broken even as he still tumbled down the hillside.

When at last he lay still, he first felt at his side for the pouch. It was still there with the precious four Little Men.

"Ah, good," he said, and then he felt the sharp pain in his leg. He raised his head to look, and he could see that it was broken. It was twisted in a strange and unnatural direction. There was no bone sticking out, however, and the skin was not broken. It was not as bad as it might have been.

The rest of his body was sore from bumps and bruises, but he was reasonably certain that nothing more was broken. He knew that he could not stand, and he knew that he had to get himself home. He looked around for something within his reach that he might use as a crutch or a staff, a cane even, but he could see nothing that would do.

Well, there was nothing for it but to crawl on his belly. He turned himself over, and the pain that shot through his body caused him to shout again out loud. He lay there for a moment, breathing deeply, letting the sharp pain subside back into a dull ache. Then with his two hands and his one good leg, he began to pull and push his way across the ground. It would be a long trip back to Kituwah.

There were no sentries looking out over the walls which surrounded Kituwah. There had been no reason of late to worry about attack from any of the neighboring peoples. But a young boy, perhaps eight or ten years old, climbed one of the long notched poles which leaned against the wall on the inside. It was just something to do.

He climbed the pole and looked over the wall. Perhaps he imagined that he was a sentry in time of war, and he was watching for the enemy's approach. When he saw the enemy coming, he would shout the alarm and save the town. Then when the actual attack came, he would climb down from the pole and fight, and he would earn a man's name, a warrior's name, and he would be a hero to the people of Kituwah. Perhaps he would fight so well that his tale would be told in other towns, and he would be known to all of the Real People throughout their widespread towns.

He stared off down the road for a while, and then he looked to his right toward Long Man, the river. He watched that way for a moment. He turned his head back toward the road and then to his left toward the high mountains. He was about to turn again toward the road when he thought he saw something unusual. He stared hard, and the thing he saw moved a bit.

He strained his eyes until he was sure, and then he yelled. It was almost as if he were sounding the alarm.

"Someone is coming," he cried. "A man is coming. He's crawling along the ground. Out there. Toward the mountains. He's coming."

A man scaled a nearby pole and took a look. Then he dropped to the ground. By then others had gathered around.

"Someone's hurt," he said.

Several of them ran through the passageway formed by the overlapping parallel ends of the wall which circled the town. They ran through until they had reached the outside, and then they ran toward the lone figure crawling along the ground. As they got close, someone recognized him.

"It's Dancing Rabbit," he said.

Dancing Rabbit heard them, and he stopped crawling. He rolled over onto his back. He could scarcely believe that he had made it. As his friends and neighbors gathered around him, he looked up into their faces, and he smiled.

"My leg is broken," he said. "Take me to White Tobacco."

Two

CARRIER HAD ALL of his trade goods laid out neatly on the ground there in front of his mother Walnut's house, the house which he shared with her and her brother, his uncle Dancing Rabbit. There had been only the three of them there since the death of Carrier's father some years earlier. He looked over his wares with pride and satisfaction. It was a good supply, and he was well pleased with it. He had collected dozens of pipes, pipes made of white clay and pipes carved from the soft gray stone, pipes made by the best pipe makers among his people, *Ani-yunwi-ya*, the Real People. These finely wrought pieces, many bearing figures of humans or of other creatures, some plain and simple, with cane stems, had always been among the most popular items he and his uncle carried to other people in faraway places.

He had other things, too: some of the soft stone, yet uncarved; mica, some pounded into sheets, some raw. He had baskets made by women of the Real People. No one else made them quite the same way as they did. He had small wood carvings by Doya, the Beaver, the renowned local carver. And this time, in addition to the locally produced goods, he had other, more exotic items, things he and his uncle had acquired from people to the north and from people to the west. From the west he had chunks of raw lead and from the north copper and even some of the rare red stone, the other soft stone with which pipe makers liked to work. These things would be especially attractive to the people in the south, and that was where Carrier was planning to go, to the south, far south to the people he knew as Timucua, south of the land of the Apalachee People. Along the way, he thought, he might stop and trade with the Oconee and the Hitchiti, but he wasn't sure about that. He wanted to be sure to have plenty with which to deal among the Timucuas.

He thought that it would be wise to try to avoid any contact with his nearer neighbors, the *Ani-Cusa* and the *Ani-Chahta*. Those two groups were not at present on friendly terms with the Real People. Besides, he thought that he would do much better with this particular batch of goods farther from home, farther south.

Carrier was more than a bit apprehensive about this trip. It would be his first time out alone. He had started traveling with his uncle, Dancing Rabbit, when he himself was still a child with his childhood name of Gnat. He had grown up with this trading business and had earned his man's name, Carrier, as a result of it.

Now he was twenty-two years old, tall and handsome. He didn't resemble his uncle in any physical way. Dancing Rabbit was short, stocky and possessed of an overly large head with a round and puffy face. Before he had earned his name of Dancing Rabbit, he had been called by the teasing nickname of Iya-Iyusti, Like-a-Pumpkin.

But Carrier fancied that he was like his mother's brother in other ways, in ways that really counted much more than mere physical appearance. Dancing Rabbit had always been his favorite uncle, and for as long as Carrier could remember, he had wanted to grow up to be just like Dancing Rabbit.

He knew that he would miss his uncle on this trip. He would miss his company and his advice. But Dancing Rabbit had only recently suffered a bad fall on the hillside outside of town and had broken his leg. It would be some time before he would be able to travel again. Carrier didn't like to think it, but perhaps Dancing Rabbit would never travel again. The break was a serious one, and Dancing Rabbit was no longer a young man. Even with the expert care and treatment of old White Tobacco, Dancing Rabbit might, at best, only hobble around for the rest of his life.

So Carrier's anxiety was twofold. It was not just that he would be traveling and trading alone for the first time. It would also, and more importantly, be the first time that the entire responsibility for the success of the venture would be, along with the bundle of goods he would be carrying, entirely on his own back. He wanted desperately to do well. He wanted his uncle to be proud of him. He wanted that more than anything else in his life.

He rolled out the large woven mat and began packing the goods to roll into a bundle. The breakable items he wrapped individually in small skins and stuffed into the baskets. When the bundle was all done up and ready to be strapped onto his back, he went into the house. Dancing Rabbit was stretched out on a cot against one of the walls, his broken leg splinted and wrapped tightly with long strips of rawhide.

"Everything is packed, Uncle," said Carrier.

"Good," said Dancing Rabbit. "I wish I was going with you, but I knew, of course, that the time would come when you would be going out on your own. It just came a little sooner than I had thought, that's all. You'll do well."

"You've trained me well, Uncle."

"Avoid the *Ani-Cusa* and the *Ani-Chahta.*"

"Yes, Uncle, I will."

"You might do well to avoid most people on your way down. That way you'll save most of your goods for the Timucuas."

"Yes, Uncle," said Carrier. Inwardly, he smiled. The advice his uncle was giving him consisted of things he had already thought of himself. That little fact gave him more confidence.

"Keep as much as possible to the high mountain roads," said Dancing Rabbit. "You'll be safer there, but keep on your guard just the same. Don't let anyone catch you by surprise."

"Don't worry, Uncle," said Carrier with a smile now showing on his face. "I had a good teacher. The best. I know the way, and I know how to travel safely. I also know with whom to trade, and I know how to keep from being cheated."

Dancing Rabbit smiled back briefly at his nephew, then looked thoughtful, even solemn for a moment, staring at the hard-packed dirt floor of the house.

"I'm a little worried about something," he said. "These rumors we've heard about the strange people who came over the waters, these men with white skin and hairy faces. They say that these men are there in the south."

"I think that I'd like to see these strange men," said Carrier, "if they're real. Everyone I've heard talk about them says only that he heard about them from someone else. No one I've heard talking even claims to have actually seen them."

"Well, if they are real, we don't know anything about them."

"Some have said that they have many wonderful things, things that we have never seen before. Very hard and sharp knives. Shirts that arrows cannot penetrate. Strange animals like big dogs on which they ride. Maybe I could trade with them for some of those things."

Carrier chuckled, but Dancing Rabbit still wore a serious expression on his large round face.

"Carrier," he said, "if you see these men, if they are real, keep your distance from them. Watch them carefully before you get close to them. If you find that they're not dangerous, then you can try to trade with them. But first watch them from a distance."

"Yes, Uncle," said Carrier. "I will."

Dancing Rabbit, somewhat clumsily, shifted himself slightly on the cot, then settled back with a long sigh.

"So when will you leave?" he said.

"I'm ready to go now."

"Your mother went to the river. She'll want to see you before you leave."

"Yes, Uncle. I'll go to her."

Carrier turned to leave the house. As he ducked to go through the doorway, Dancing Rabbit stopped him.

"Nephew," he said.

Carrier turned back toward his uncle.

"Yes?"

Dancing Rabbit's next words were spoken in a low whisper, as if he were afraid of being overheard.

"Don't neglect to study the writing."

Carrier gave a nod.

"*Do-na-da-go-huh-i,*" he said.

"Yes," said Dancing Rabbit. "We shall see one another again."

Having taken leave of his mother, Carrier, the large bundle strapped to his back and a long staff in hand, walked out beyond the walls of the town and climbed the steep mountain trail which would lead him eventually to the land to the south. When he reached the crest of the mountain, he unburdened himself, laid aside his weapons and his staff and opened a small pouch which was hanging around his neck. He brought a small clay pipe out of the pouch and then filled its bowl with tobacco, also from the pouch. The mixture had been given to him by the old man White Tobacco, and had been specially prepared for this occasion.

"To protect you on your journey," the old man had said.

Carrier smoked the tobacco there on top of the mountain. He turned and smoked it toward each of the four directions. He smoked in silence. There was nothing to be said. White Tobacco, in his elaborate preparations, had already said it all. The ceremony done, Carrier put the pipe away, strapped the pack on once again, picked up his weapons and his staff and resumed his journey.

Dancing Rabbit was alone in the house. He had confidence in his nephew, for he knew that the young man was capable. The two of them had traveled the route together before, more than once. Carrier knew the way. He knew the people he would encounter and with whom he would deal. He had learned the trade well. He was a bright young man and a quick learner.

He had proved the quickness of his mind when Dancing Rabbit had chosen him as a young boy still known as Gnat to be the caretaker of the writing. Dancing Rabbit recalled his own days as Like-a-Pumpkin, the scribe-priest, the *Kutani*. He and a few others had been the keepers of the records and the sacred writings. The writing had been considered so sacred that it had been kept secret from the general population of the Real People, although some had suspected its existence.

Then the people had risen up against the *Ani-Kutani* and

had very nearly killed them all. Dancing Rabbit lived only because he had been away at the time of the attack. He had only come upon the scene at the conclusion of the bloodletting. There might be one other *Kutani* yet living, one of his traveling companions from those days, a man called Deadwood Lighter, but if Deadwood Lighter still lived, he was a miserable captive somewhere far to the west, and Deadwood Lighter had not been a scribe. That meant that Dancing Rabbit had been the only person alive in the whole world who knew the writing.

Because of a deep-seated fear of the people's old hatred for the *Ani-Kutani*, a fear that it could yet rise up again, Dancing Rabbit felt a need to keep his own knowledge of the writing a secret. Yet he retained a strong belief in the importance, in the sacredness of the writing, and the thought that it could vanish without a trace upon his death horrified him. He had therefore impressed upon the young Gnat the importance both of the writing itself and of the need for absolute secrecy regarding it, and he had taught the system to the boy.

And that was another reason he worried. If anything should happen to Carrier on this trip, his first alone, Dancing Rabbit would not only lose his nephew and Walnut her son, but the writing, the sacred writing, would be forever lost. It would die with Dancing Rabbit, for he could not think of another person he could trust the way he trusted his nephew.

Ah, he thought, why was I so foolish as to fall and break my leg?

Just then his sister appeared in the doorway. She ducked her head to come inside, and she placed a jug of fresh water there just inside the doorway.

"Well," she said, "he's gone."

"Don't worry about Carrier," said Dancing Rabbit. "He's grown. He knows what he's doing. He'll make the trip to the south and back with no problems. I have absolute confidence in his abilities and his judgment."

But, he thought, if these strangers we've heard about are real, and he comes upon them, he has no experience with them. What might they be like? Men with white skin and hairy faces. Men with shirts that an arrow cannot go through, riding upon the backs of great dogs. Ah well, perhaps my nephew is right. Perhaps these strange men do not really even exist. As he said, no one seems to have seen them. Those who carry the rumors have only heard others tell about them. Perhaps they're not real at all.

M. J.

Three

I T TOOK SEVERAL DAYS of traveling for Carrier to
get through the land of his own people, the Real People, and each time he came to a town, he stopped to rest
and to visit. He did not intend to trade with his own people. During the times between their long trading trips, he
and his uncle did their local trading among the Real People. In spite of that, there were almost always some in
those towns who wanted to trade, and Carrier would feel
obliged to accommodate them. He made one or two small
trades in each town of the Real People he stopped at. Then
he began to deliberately avoid the towns. He couldn't afford to take a chance on trading away his best wares before
his trip was really even started.

Then he came to the country of the *Ani-Cusa*, the people
who called themselves Muskogee, the people immediately
to the south of his own people. They were a numerous
people with a vast domain, almost rivaling that of the Real
People. The *Ani-Cusa* themselves were not so numerous as

were the Real People, but they had taken a number of smaller groups in with them to form a large and powerful confederacy. Among them were Alabamas, Koasatis, Hitchitis, Yuchis, Okmulgees, Sawoklis, Chiahas, Tuskegees and others.

He knew that he would have to travel through the land of the *Ani-Cusa* with extreme caution. There had been no open hostilities between the two peoples in recent times, but they were not friendly with one another, and they had never formally made peace. It was entirely possible, he knew, that if he ran across any *Ani-Cusa* who happened to be in the wrong mood, they would kill him and take all his goods. It was equally possible that they might only want to trade, but he did not want to take a chance, did not want to find out the hard way.

It was when he began traveling through the land of the *Ani-Cusa* that he started to really miss the company of Dancing Rabbit. He had no one with whom to talk, no one to help make the decisions. And if he should run into trouble, he would have to face it all alone.

He had known all that, of course, before he began the journey. And he had said that he could easily handle it alone. He had looked forward to the responsibility, to the boldness of it, in fact, as a way of proving himself a man. Yet there was a difference in knowing it before the fact and experiencing it all alone, day after day, and night after lonely night. He told himself he would be all right. He would reach the land to the south beside the big water there, and he would make good trades with the Timucua People there. He might even see the strange white, hairy-faced people with hard shirts and trade with them for whatever exotic items they might have. He hoped they would like his goods.

He imagined a scene in which he had just returned home with unusual and useful items obtained from these strangers. Everyone would gather around in amazement to see what he had brought. Perhaps he might even acquire one of the big animals on which it was said the strangers rode. He wondered if he would be able to climb on its back and ride it. Ah, he thought, that would really amaze them back home.

He imagined a scene in which he had just ridden into Kituwah on the back of a strange beast. The people of the town were all gathered around, staring openmouthed. He was wearing one of the strange shirts, and some of the people began throwing rocks at him. He laughed as the rocks bounced off his chest.

For several days Carrier managed to avoid any contact with the *Ani-Cusa*, and he was deep in their territory when he made a camp for the night. It was a simple camp. He built a small fire, and he ate a simple trail meal. Then he spread a long cloak out on the ground beside his pack and stretched out on his back. It was a clear night, and up above he saw all the stars shining brightly in the sky. He wondered if they were really like the little creatures described in the old story, and to amuse himself and to help himself sleep, he told the old tale over again in his mind.

It had been long ago. Some hunters had been out on the trail a long ways from home. They made a small camp, and when night fell, they noticed along a nearby ridge two lights running along on the ground.

The next night they saw the lights again. They were curious and wondered what the lights might be. They saw the lights again the third night and again the fourth, and that night they said, "Let's go up there in the morning and see

if we can discover what those strange lights might be."
They all agreed.

When the sun came out in the morning, the hunters climbed the mountain and reached the ridge. After a short search, they came upon two small creatures. The creatures were not as tall as the men, but they were absolutely round, and they were covered with what appeared to be gray fur. But when the wind blew and ruffled the fur, sparks flew out from it.

The hunters captured the two strange creatures and planned to take them home to show the other people. The creatures did not resist. They did nothing, in fact, until dark when they began to glow. The hunters traveled toward home with their prizes until they had camped six times and traveled for seven days. Then they camped for the seventh time.

The creatures had given them no trouble, had not struggled or tried to escape, but when the sun vanished on the seventh night, the creatures began to glow as they had done before, and then they began to rise slowly up from the ground. The astonished hunters watched in awe as the creatures rose higher and higher until they were two tiny dots of light in the sky, and then the men knew that they had captured, for a time, two stars.

Carrier drifted off to sleep, and the next thing he knew, it was morning. The sun was just beginning to peek out from under the eastern edge of the Sky Vault to brighten the horizon. Carrier got up and stretched. He ate a little of his dried corn and drank some water. Then he rolled up his cloak, made sure his small fire was well out, heaved the pack up on his back, took up his staff and resumed his journey.

The sun was halfway to her daughter's house, straight overhead, when he saw the *Ani-Cusa*. There were five of them, directly ahead, sitting around a campfire beside the trail. They had seen him, but they did not get up. They did not grab for their weapons. There was nothing for Carrier to do but continue straight ahead. He took a deep breath and walked on. When he had arrived within a few paces of the lounging *Ani-Cusa*, he spoke to them, using the trade language. At least one of them will know it, he thought.

"Hello."

"Hello," said one of the men. "You're a trader?"

"Yes."

"A Chiloki?"

"Yes. I'm known as Carrier. I come from Kituwah in the land of the Real People, the Chilokis."

It irked Carrier slightly to use the trade jargon word for his own people. It was very similar to the word used by the Choctaws to designate the Real People, and it was distasteful to him.

"What are you carrying then, Carrier?" said the *Cusa*, with a sideways smile.

Carrier smiled, working hard to appear to be as friendly as he could, and shifted the weight of the pack on his back.

"Common trade items," he said. "May I know your names?"

"I'm called Big Snake," said the *Cusa*. "These are my friends: Big Turtle, Heavy Hand, Alligator, Bobcat. Sit down here with us and rest."

Carrier hesitated a moment, then shrugged and dropped his pack to the ground and sat down beside it.

"I've only been traveling a short while this morning," he said, "but I will sit with you for a while."

Big Snake reached for the end of a spit which held suspended over the fire a piece of meat.

Yansa, thought Carrier, from the smell of it, and the inside of his mouth began to water in anticipation.

"Have the buffalo been here so recently?" he asked. "We have not seen any in my country for some time now."

"Only a few strays," said Big Snake. "Have some."

He handed the meat to Carrier, who took it and started to eat. It was good. He had been living off nothing but trail food since leaving his own country for fear of attracting attention. Now he had blundered into these *Ani-Cusa*, and they had given him some good buffalo meat to eat. He wondered if they were toying with him, if they would kill him yet. They seemed friendly enough so far, but one could never tell. They all sat silent while Carrier ate. He did not finish the meat, but he did eat his fill. Then he handed the remaining still-spitted buffalo flesh back to Big Snake.

"It's good," he said. "Thank you."

"Show us your wares, trader," said Heavy Hand.

"Yes," said Bobcat. "We may want to trade something with you."

"I was going farther south to trade," said Carrier, "but maybe we can trade something here." He started unwrapping his pack. "I'm hoping to see the strangers. Have you heard of them?"

The five *Ani-Cusa* all moved eagerly toward the pack, waiting to see what would be revealed when Carrier got it unwrapped.

"You mean the men with hairy faces?" said Big Snake.

"Yes," said Carrier, "and white skin, they say."

"I've heard that they have shirts which are so hard that arrows shatter when they hit them," said Bobcat.

"And long sharp knives," said Alligator. "And they have big animals like dogs, so big that the men can ride on their backs."

"If you had one of these strange animals, trader," said Bobcat, "you wouldn't have to carry your own pack on your back. You could tie it on the animal's back."

They all laughed at that image. Carrier looked up briefly from his work.

"Have you seen them?" he asked.

"No," said Big Snake. "We've not seen the men or the animals. We've only heard tales. I myself do not believe that they exist."

"I believe they exist," said Alligator. "I've heard several different people tell about them."

"So have I," said Heavy Hand. "But I don't know if I believe the stories or not."

Bobcat glanced toward Carrier. "What about you?" he asked. "Do you believe that these hairy faces exist?"

"I don't know," said Carrier, "but I hope that they do. I'd like to trade for one of the big animals and maybe some of the long knives and the hard shirts."

He laid open the pack, and immediately Big Snake reached for the obsidian knife. Carrier's heart fell. It was one of his prize items for this trip. But still he was not completely comfortable with these *Ani-Cusa*. He had to be careful of anything he said.

"What will you take for this?" said Big Snake. "I need this. I broke my own knife just this morning."

"Take it from me as a gift," said Carrier. Then before anyone had time to make any other suggestions, he gathered up four of the carved black pipes and handed them to the other men. "And these for you," he said. "Now, do you still want to trade for something else?"

There was a long pause. The five *Ani-Cusa* looked at one another. Then Big Snake spoke.

"You said before that you didn't really want to trade yet."

"I want to look for these strangers and see if I can trade with them," said Carrier, "but I'm willing to trade with you."

"No," said Big Snake. "Take your goods on farther south. If you do find these strange white men, get a big dog and a hard shirt and a long knife. When you're on your way back home, stop and see us again and show us those things. That way, we'll know once and for all if they're real."

"Better yet," said Heavy Hand, "catch one of the white-faced, hairy men and lead him here on a rope, so we can see him."

They all laughed at that image.

"Where will I find you?" asked Carrier.

"Don't worry, trader," said Big Snake. "When you're on your way back through our country, we'll know about it. We'll find you."

Carrier was in the land of the *Ani-Cusa* for several more days, but he had no more trouble with them, no more encounters. He wondered if Big Snake had spread the word to all the others to leave him alone so that he could find out about the strangers for them. If so, that was all right with Carrier. The only problem then would be the attitude of Big Snake on Carrier's return trip. Suppose Carrier was successful. Suppose he did actually find the strangers. Then on his way home he would be stopped again by these men, and he would tell them what he had seen. Then what? Would they be appreciative for the information and let him go in peace? Would that satisfy them? Or would they, having learned what they wanted from him, kill him? Well, he would worry about that when the time came. He still had a long journey south to make. There would be plenty of time to consider strategies for the return trip through the land of the *Ani-Cusa*.

Four

H E WAS CALLED DOYA, or Beaver, because, like
the beaver, he was known for his skill at cutting
wood, or perhaps because, also like the beaver, he had promi-
nent upper front teeth. Perhaps it was for both reasons. At
any rate, Doya was a carver of wood. He cut masks from
usquada, the buckeye, spoons and ladles from *tsiyu*, the yellow poplar, walking sticks from *wanei*, the hickory. He was
highly respected, and his products were sought after and
cherished.

Dancing Rabbit was well pleased, therefore, when Doya
brought him a new, specially fashioned crutch. Doya had
made it from *kalogwek'di*, locust wood, and it was exactly the
right length for Dancing Rabbit. The staff of the crutch was so
straight that it seemed almost perfect, but at the top, the wood
turned three times in order to form a triangle, its top section
carefully wrapped with rabbit skins for padding.

Dancing Rabbit thanked Doya profusely. He praised the
workmanship that had created such a fine crutch, and he paid

the craftsman well with a quantity of ancient, or sacred, tobacco, *tsola gayunli*.

"Well then," said Doya, "go ahead and try it out."

"Yes," said Dancing Rabbit. "Of course."

He was sitting on the cot, his bound, broken leg sticking straight out in front of him. He hesitated a moment, then, holding the crutch in both of his hands, planted it firmly on the hard, dirt floor. He took a deep breath and pulled himself up on his good leg. He put the crutch under his arm and leaned on it, weaving only a little. He smiled a tentative smile.

"It's good," he said. "Strong."

"Walk on it," said Doya through a broad grin, beaming with the pride of an artist.

Dancing Rabbit shifted his weight to his good leg and moved the stick ahead, leaned heavily on it again, then hopped forward on his good leg. He repeated the procedure until he had worked his way slowly across the small room to the wall on the other side. Then, panting from the effort, he managed to turn himself around. He was still smiling, but less tentatively than before.

"That's good," said Doya. "But don't try to do too much of that right away. Well, I'll leave you now."

It was a slow and tedious process, but after having been confined to the cot in the house for so long, Dancing Rabbit felt as if he had been given a new freedom along with the new crutch. He practiced until he became skillful at his new gait and until the strength in his good leg was built up again. Soon he was hobbling all around the town to look at things, to visit with people, but mainly he wandered aimlessly just to be moving. Occasionally he would hop all the way outside the walls of Kituwah and gaze southward, wondering about his nephew.

He wondered how far away from home Carrier had gotten by this time, and how many places he had stopped along the way to visit. He wondered about the people Carrier had visited thus far. Were they people that he, too, knew? Where might Carrier be at just this moment? Had he run into any problems, and, if so, how had he handled them? And, of course, he wondered if Carrier would actually see any of the strangers about whom they had heard so many stories. He hoped not. He hoped that the strangers did not really exist.

At those times, he also felt just a little guilty about his broken leg. I should have been more careful, he would think. But then he would tell himself that it was probably all for the best, that Carrier needed the experience in order to prove himself a man, that this had all been meant to happen in just this way. And he would remind himself that Carrier was well prepared for his journey. He was young, strong and healthy. He was intelligent. He knew the way, and he was well trained. Everything would work out for the best.

Potmaker peered out from behind a tree in astonishment at the two huge vessels which approached the coastline. She was not alone. Almost all of the people from her village were hiding there in the vicinity and watching. They had heard of the people who traveled in these boats from the Calusa, their neighbors to the south, but they had not before seen them for themselves. The Timucuas, Potmaker's people, knew what the vessels were when they saw them. They knew from the descriptions they had been given. Even so, they were not prepared for the actual sight of the great boats. They watched in combined amazement and fear as the dreadful vessels drew closer to land.

"They are coming here," shouted Shark Tooth from a hiding place not far from Potmaker's. She could not see him, but she recognized his voice. She had heard it often enough, for he had been pursuing her for some time now, trying to talk her into marriage.

"What shall we do?" came another voice, this one from a little farther away and not readily identifiable to Potmaker.

The Timucuas had heard tales of the ferocity of these strange men from across the waters. They came in their big boats, and they disembarked with their huge dog-like beasts. From one big boat would come perhaps a hundred men, and some of them would be riding upon the backs of the beasts. The bodies of the men would be almost completely covered with clothing, strange clothing, some of which was made of a very hard metal, and their faces were mostly hidden by hair. What little skin that showed through was pale, almost white.

Then they would attack. They would ride into crowds of people on the backs of the great beasts, and people would be trampled by the hard feet of the beasts. The men would slash at the people with their long, sharp knives, or run them through with long, hard, sharp-pointed lances.

And they had other weapons that none of the people had ever seen before. They had weapons made like tubes, like blowguns, but made of the hard metal, and these weapons made a loud noise and spat fire and sent little hard pieces of metal flying at their victims. Some of these weapons were small. The hairy-faced men carried them in their arms. Others were large and mounted on great wheels. These had to be pulled or pushed along the ground.

Potmaker and her people had heard all of these things from the Calusas who lived to the south. They had heard that these strangers would attack and kill, or that they would capture people to carry away into slavery in some faraway place. Those who were carried away were never heard from again, the Calusas said. The Timucuas of Potmaker's village did not want these frightful strangers landing in their country.

The big boats came in even closer, and the Timucuas could hear the men on board shouting back and forth at each other. The harsh noises, of course, made no sense to the Timucuas. Then Shark Tooth suddenly and boldly emerged from his hiding place. Nearly naked, his body was totally covered with tattoos, emblems of his many war deeds. Feathered earplugs adorned his ears, and his arms, legs and waist were banded with strings of mussel shells, alternately dark and light. From a cord around his neck a large conch shell hung down over his sternum, and on his head was a cap of otter skin profusely decorated with a variety of brightly colored feathers.

Shark Tooth stepped out upon the bare beach in full view of the strangers in the boats. He stood bravely for a moment alone, then he waved his long warclub menacingly over his head. The club was carved from wood and had embedded along one edge a row of shark's teeth.

"Go away," he shouted. "Do not stop here. You're not welcome here."

Then four more Timucua men stepped out of hiding to stand just behind Shark Tooth. They too shouted defiantly.

"Go back where you came from."

"If you step on our land, we'll fight you. We'll kill you."

"You'll get no slaves here. We'll fight you and die first. We Timucuas are not slaves to any man."

From the boats, hairy-faced men returned the shouts and wild gestures, and the boats moved even closer to the shore. They were close enough that Potmaker could see the faces of the men, and they were even more horrible than she had imagined. Some of the men had their metal hats on, but others did not. The faces she saw were not really white, as she had heard, but ruddy, an unhealthy color. And she saw hair that was red and hair that was nearly white, hair of almost every color, and almost all the faces she saw were covered with hair. She was not sure that these were really men. If they were men, they were not like any men she had ever seen.

The men, if men they were, on the near boat seemed to be having some sort of discussion, and then they pushed forward one man who then stood alone near the wall at the edge of the big boat. She realized that he did not look like the others. He was not dressed as they were. His breast was bare. And his skin was brown. His hair black. He held up his arms as if asking for attention, and he shouted, and he spoke in the language of the Timucuas.

"Listen to me," he shouted.

The people on the beach, amazed to hear their own language coming from the big boat, stood quietly to listen to what was said. The man on the boat, with a hairy-faced man standing right beside him, continued.

"I used to be called He-Fights-with-Alligators when I lived with my own people, your neighbors, the Calusas. These people I am with now are called Españols. I'm talking for them.

"They told me to say these things. Don't be afraid. They have not come to fight with you. They want to be your friends, they say. They are coming on shore now, whether you like it or not. You'll run for your lives if you know what's good for you."

"They don't understand what he's saying," said one of the men. "He's warned us to run away."

"I'm not afraid of any man," said Shark Tooth. "Give me your bow."

The man nearest Shark Tooth handed him a bow and an arrow. Shark Tooth nocked the arrow and pulled back the string. He let the arrow fly, and it traveled in a high arc, then fell into the water just short of the big boat. Other Timucuas came out of the brush and began shooting arrows at the boats. Some reached the boat. None struck any of the men on board.

Then one of the white men aimed one of the firing tubes. There was an explosion, a belching of fire and smoke. The Timucuas who had exposed themselves, all, including Shark Tooth, ran for cover.

"What do we do now?" someone called out.

"Stay and fight," said Shark Tooth.

"There are old people in the village," shouted Potmaker from her hiding place, "and children. It's all right if you want to stand here and fight and maybe die, but what if the strangers fight their way through you and go on to the village? What will happen then?"

"Let's all go back to the village," said someone.

"All right, the rest of you go back," said Shark Tooth. "I'll stay here to see what the hairy faces do. Get the children and the old ones ready to abandon the village. If the strangers head for the village, I'll run and tell you."

Potmaker was one of the first to reach the village, and she and all those behind her were shouting at once. The people in the village came out of their houses to see what was going on.

"The white, hairy-faced strangers are at the beach in two big boats," said Potmaker. "They're coming ashore. Shark Tooth has stayed behind to see what they're going to do. We have to get out of here and hide in case they come this way."

"Hurry," someone shouted. "Hurry."

"Find your children."

"Help the old people."

Children screamed and dogs barked and people seemed to

be running in all directions at once. Then suddenly Shark Tooth appeared on the scene.

"They are coming this way," he said, "and they're riding the big dogs. We have to abandon the village."

And remarkably, in a matter of a few moments, the village was abandoned. Not a dog was left to bark.

Five

CARRIER WAS AT LAST in the land of the Apalachees. He had passed by three Apalachee villages, carefully keeping his presence a secret. So far he had not been seen by anyone in this country. He was not afraid of the Apalachees. He simply did not want to trade with them, and it was easier to avoid them altogether than to refuse any approaches they might make.

He had found himself a good spot to spend the night, high on a little-traveled mountain trail near a clear-running, cold mountain stream. He built himself a small, almost smokeless fire. Then he took a cooking pot out of his pack and dipped some water into it from the stream. He set the pot over the fire and added some of his *guhwisida*. He was tired of eating the parched corn meal dry.

It was not yet dark, and the *guhwisida* would not be ready for a while. Carrier leaned back on one elbow, and, with a stick, he began to draw in the dirt. He drew the characters that spelled his name. Then he spelled the name of his uncle,

Dancing Rabbit. He rubbed those out and wrote in the dirt, "I am alone. I'm going south alone. I'm going to trade with the Timucua people." He rubbed out those words and started again. This time he wrote, "I am going to see the men with hairy faces."

He rubbed out the last of his writing, and he ate his hot *guhwisida*. Then he washed out the pot and replaced it in the pack, and he stretched out on the ground to try to get a good night's sleep.

The next day when the sun had almost reached her daughter's house directly overhead, Carrier stopped walking. He stood a moment thinking. Ahead was one more Apalachee town. Not far beyond that was the end of the Apalachee territory. Tomorrow he would reach the land of the Timucuas. But he would not likely see any people for another day or two. He was craving some hot food, some fresh cooked meat. He decided that he would go down into the Apalachee town. If he had to trade some with the Apalachees, so be it. He would trade.

The sun had finished her visit with her daughter and had begun her descent toward the west. She had not yet gotten far from her daughter's house, though. Carrier walked into the Apalachee town. He called out a greeting in the trade language and identified himself. A man perhaps the age of his uncle came forward smiling.

"Hello, Carrier," he said. "Welcome. We haven't seen you for a long time. Where's Dancing Rabbit?"

"Dancing Rabbit is at home with a broken leg," said Carrier. "I'm alone this trip."

"Come over to my house and eat," said the Apalachee. "Then we'll visit."

They fed him fresh venison and beans and corn, and Carrier

ate until he could eat no more. It was the best meal he had eaten since leaving the country of his own people.

"So, Carrier," said his host, "did you come to trade with us?"

This was the part of the visit to the Apalachee town that Carrier had been dreading. He had known that it would come, and he had decided that he wanted a good meal badly enough to deal with it. He would have to be shrewd with these Apalachees.

"No," he said. "I didn't come to trade with you. I just stopped to visit, to see old friends. I don't think that I have anything in my pack that you would want. I'm on my way to see the Timucuas, your neighbors to the south. They're not as rich as you are, so they might be interested in the things I have."

"Let's see what you have. We might be interested in something."

Others had gathered around by that time, and they joined in.

"Yes, Carrier. Open your pack for us."

"I have some good furs which I might be willing to trade."

"I have some things at my house. I'll go get them and bring them right back. Wait for me while I run to get them."

Carrier reluctantly opened his pack and spread out his goods. He was not enthusiastic. He wondered what his uncle would think of him for getting himself into this fix. Had the meal been worth it? Well, he was going to have to trade. He would be as shrewd as he knew how to be and try to come out ahead. Maybe it would all work out for the best after all.

When it was all over, those things which he had considered to be his best items were gone, but he had bargained sternly with them and had received more than what they were worth in the more common items which the Apalachees had offered.

His pack would be larger than before and heavier. He wondered again about the large animals the strangers were supposed to have. It would be nice to have a large animal to carry the pack for him.

He was wrapping his goods up again. Some of the Apalachee people were going home with their new acquisitions. They all seemed to be pleased with the outcome of the trading.

"Be careful going south," said his host.

Carrier looked up inquisitively.

"Of what should I be careful?" he asked.

"The white men," said the Apalachee. "They seem to be coming around more and more. There seems to be no end to them."

"These—white men," said Carrier. "Has anyone actually seen them? People always tell me that someone else has seen them. I have never yet met anyone who says that he himself saw them."

"I have seen them, Carrier, and they are horrible to look at. They're hairy all over their bodies and their faces, and their hair comes in all colors. Their skin is pale, nearly white, but there's a redness that shows through, almost as if you can see the blood beneath the skin showing through. I think their skin is very thin. And they have eyes of every color, too: blue and green, watery-looking."

Carrier had stopped fooling with his pack. The Apalachee suddenly had all of his wide-eyed attention. This was indeed interesting. Here was a man who claimed that he had actually seen the strangers. Carrier felt sudden anxious curiosity. At last he felt as if he was getting close to the strangers he so longed to see, to find out about, hopefully to trade with.

"Where did you see them?" he asked.

"Not far from here. To the west, but on the coast. They

come from somewhere in very large boats, and they ride in these boats all along the coastline. They have given this land, my land and the land of the Timucuas and the land of the Calusas even farther to the south, they have given this land a name as if they believe that it's their own land. I heard the name said, but I can't remember it. I remember that I couldn't pronounce it anyway. Their language is very strange, just like everything else about them.

"Anyway, I was there to the southwest visiting the relatives of my wife, and we saw the boats. Three of them. We went to the beach to meet the strangers, and they came ashore. They were ugly and frightening, but they seemed to be friendly enough, so we invited them to the village. They came with us and ate, and then they went back to their boats. The boats stayed there in the water all night.

"The next morning they brought their big riding animals off the boats, maybe twenty-four or twenty-five of them, and men were on their backs. They wore metal shirts and hats, and they carried large metal shields in front of them. They rode into the village, and the people all ran from them. They were frightened of the animals. But the strangers killed three of the people with their long lances and one with one of the loud shooting sticks. They captured two alive and took them away. We hid in the forest for a long time, until the strangers got back into their boats and went away.

"Yes. I've seen them, and I hope I never see them again. But I'm afraid that I will. I'm afraid they'll be back. They keep coming. More and more of them. All along the coast."

"Did no one try to kill these men?" asked Carrier, somewhat disgusted at the thought of people running away from men who were killing some of their number and carrying some others away.

"Some of the men shot arrows at them, but the arrows shattered on the metal shirts and shields."

"I had been hoping to see them," said Carrier, after a thoughtful pause. "I thought that they might trade with me."

"If you see them, Carrier, run. They won't trade with you. They'll steal all that you have. Then they'll either kill you or take you away with them to be a slave. No one knows where they take their captives. No one ever sees them again."

"Have they been here," said Carrier, "to your village?"

"No. Not yet."

Carrier busied himself securing his bundle of wares, but he was deep in thought. The things he had just heard were frightening, horrible to contemplate, yet he couldn't help himself. He was, if anything, more curious than ever about these strangers. When he had finished with his bundle, he sat on the ground and leaned an arm on the large pack.

"You fed them," he said. "They were your guests, and yet they attacked you."

"That's true."

"What kind of men are these?"

And the question was more than rhetorical. Carrier wanted to know the answer. His head was full of questions about these strange men. Where had they come from, he wondered. And what were they doing here? What was it about them that caused them to behave the way they did? What kind of man would accept hospitality from another and then kill him or carry him away into slavery? And still he wondered about their strange and wonderful-sounding possessions.

"What were their big animals like?" he asked. "Some have said they're like big dogs."

"No," said the other. "They're not like big dogs. I would say that they're more like big deer. But the males don't have antlers."

"And the men ride on them?"

"On some of them. On others they put things. Like your bundle there. These big animals carry things on their backs. Maybe men. Maybe other things."

What a thing that would be, thought Carrier, to have a big animal to walk along beside me with my bundle on his back. Again his mind conjured up an image of his return to Kituwah. He saw himself walking into the town with one of the big animals beside him. On its back was his bundle of new trade goods, and in the bundle were shirts and shields and knives of metal. In his arms he carried a shooting tube. The people would all be amazed. Dancing Rabbit would be proud, and perhaps even a little jealous.

Well, it was late in the afternoon. He would spend the night here with these Apalachees, and early in the morning he would head out for the country of the Timucuas. In less than two days, he would arrive at his destination, the Timucua village he had visited before with his uncle. It was a place where he was known, and it was a place where they had made good trades in the past.

When Carrier had walked just a short distance away from the Apalachee town, he felt more alone than he had at any time before on this journey, perhaps more than any time before in his life. He found himself watching over his shoulder, looking ahead carefully in anticipation of likely spots for ambush. Images of the fearful strangers were dancing through his mind, and thoughts of sudden, violent death or dreadful captivity troubled him. He kept his weapons ready, easy to grasp in a hurry.

The Timucuas were his friends and trading partners, but these strangers were another matter altogether. The tales he had heard, especially those recent ones in the Apalachee town, had indeed frightened him, even horrified him. He couldn't imagine anything worse than coming upon the strangers unawares. As a child he had been frightened by tales of the dreaded *uk'ten'*, the giant mythical snake with antlers like a deer and wings like a bird, the monster whose breath could kill, but he no longer believed those tales, or if he believed them, he believed that the monsters had lived long ago and were no longer around.

These new monsters were very real and could very easily be somewhere near. Carrier was still curious, still wanted to see them, even to trade with them if such was at all possible. But with his new information, he wanted to see the strangers before they saw him, wanted the opportunity to study them from a safe hiding place, wanted to approach them, if at all, in his own time and on his own terms.

He found himself stopping often to study the lay of the land ahead and to listen for any unusual sounds. He would not be at the Timucua village as soon as he had thought. The extra care he was taking would add time to the trip. It might also make the difference between getting there and dying somewhere along the way.

Six

POTMAKER AND SIX OTHERS of her people, including her older brother, Tree Frog, headed together for another Timucua village for shelter. The rest of the people of their village split up into similar-sized groups, and each group headed for a different village. There were two reasons for this: it would be easier for each village to give support to only a few refugees than to many, and by going in small groups to several different villages, the people of Potmaker's village would be able to spread the warning of the presence of the dangerous strangers to most, if not all, of the Timucua towns.

When the people had first scattered out of the village and into the forest, they could hear behind them the frightful clanking of the strangers' metal and the pounding of the hoofs of the big animals. Potmaker had fought off an almost uncontrollable urge to slow down, to look back and see what was happening in her town. Like all the others, she ran ahead through the thick forest. In a while there was no more noise from behind. For the time being, at least, there was apparently no more pursuit. The strangers must have stopped chasing them and gone back to the abandoned village. Potmaker wondered whether they would move in there to live or just destroy the village. She was certain that they would not simply go away and leave it as they had found it.

Carrier was at long last in the land of the Timucua people. He was weary from his long journey and from worry, and he was still, he thought, about a half a day's walk from the village that was his destination. He was still nervous, too, but not quite so much as he had been just after leaving the Apalachee village with the dreadful images of the strangers yet fresh in his mind. He still watched the trail ahead, and he still looked back over his shoulder frequently. He would be glad to reach his destination and to have the comfort of old acquaintances and the strength of numbers around him once again.

He was close enough that he was beginning to feel almost triumphant. He had just about completed the long journey alone, a journey through sometimes dangerous territory. With the exception of his one foolish blunder into the lounging *Ani-Cusa* around their small campfire, he had successfully avoided people when he wanted to avoid them. And he had even managed the one unintentional encounter with the *Ani-Cusa* nicely enough. As soon as he reached the Timucua village, before nightfall, he would be almost half done with his job. Some trading. A little time for rest. Then the return.

He was feeling ambivalent regarding the strangers by this time. He was still curious, of course, still wanted to see them for himself and to see their clothing, weapons and animals. He wanted to be the one to bring firsthand knowledge of these men to his own people. But from what he had heard, he was more than just apprehensive about any meeting with them.

Perhaps, he thought, it would be best after all to avoid them, to trade with the Timucuas and to return very cautiously back home.

In her host village, Potmaker found herself surrounded by the curious.

"What has happened?" they asked.

"The strangers came. They came in two boats. Two big boats. Shark Tooth told them to go away. He told them they're not welcome here in our land. He and some others shot arrows, but the boats were too far out. Then from one of the boats, one of the strangers shot one of their metal tubes that spit fire and make a loud noise like thunder. We ran. We abandoned our village and split up. We few came here, and others went to other of our villages to tell them there what happened."

"Where are the strangers now?"

"We hurried away, so I'm not sure," said Potmaker, "but I think they're in our village. I don't think they tried to follow us through the forest very far."

"But if they're in your village, how long will it be before they come here? The trail leads right to us. Surely they'll find it and follow it."

"You'll have to be prepared for the worst," said Tree Frog. "They are bound to follow the trail sooner or later. They would probably have followed it sooner, but we came here through the forest. They followed us for a short while."

"We'll put men out to watch the trail."

"Not just the trail. All directions."

"We'll be ready for them."

"Ready for what? To run or to fight?"

"We'll have to decide that. For now, we'll just watch to make sure that the strangers don't come upon us by surprise."

.   .   .   .

Carrier knew that the Timucua village he sought was not far ahead. He was walking along the beach with the ocean on his right-hand side. It was hard to walk in the deep sand, but the beach way was the easiest way to the village. Up ahead not far was a trail which wound generally eastward through the forest and on to the village. He would be glad to reach his destination and to unload his burden. He would be glad again for friendly company, a warm meal and a good rest.

Then he saw ahead, seemingly out on the water, two strange large objects. He was still too far from them to make them out clearly, but they seemed to be out of place. He stopped and stared for a moment. They looked like large ducks riding lazily on the softly rolling waves. Then he moved ahead a little, cautiously, curiously. Closer, he could see the outlines. They were certainly not ducks. He could see that the objects were indeed riding on the water. They were large. He moved closer.

"The big boats," he said, and he spoke out loud, surprising himself. "The strangers. The strangers are here."

He ran away from the water to the edge of the forest, and then he began walking again toward the boats, but keeping himself in the minimal cover of the shade at the edge of the forest. Then he could see them clearly. He had never before seen any boats like them, any boats so large.

Now and then he could see men moving about on the boats, and now and then he could even hear a voice. He could not see the men clearly, nor could he hear the voices clearly. He could not be absolutely sure, but he thought that the path he sought was just about in a direct line inland from where the boats bobbed and floated on the water.

He wondered if the strangers had come ashore, if his Timucua friends had encountered them, if the strangers had gone into the Timucua village. He noticed that his heart had begun pounding faster and harder. He wondered what he should do. What, he asked himself, would Dancing Rabbit do in a situation like this?

He did not think that any of the strangers on the boats had seen him, but he also considered the possibility that some of them might be wandering around on land. If he were not careful, he might come upon them, or they him, by accident. Then he would probably have to run. His large, heavy bundle of trade goods was suddenly a serious liability. He stepped into the forest and unburdened his back. He made some effort to try to hide the bundle and to take careful note of the place so that he could retrieve it later. He hoped that he was being foolish and that his friends would laugh at him for having abandoned his goods in such a way.

Then he started moving slowly and as quietly as possible through the forest toward the village. At least he thought he was moving toward the village. He was not following a trail. The trail, he thought, was up there in view of the men on the boats.

He had gone only a few steps when he was reminded of the fact that he had not prepared himself for a walk through the dense forest, especially this far south, in this hot and sticky land with the heavy air. He was not wearing his shirt or his leggings, and the tangled brush and low branches were scratching his bare skin.

In addition, he had not painted himself, and the biting in-sects were annoying him terribly. These new bothers made him all the more anxious to find the Timucuas, and he hoped that he would discover things in their village to be normal, comfortable and quiet. If so, the first thing he would do would be to inquire about a doctor who could provide a soothing ointment for his skin.

He was beginning to wonder if he was on the right track. He was not familiar with this forest, and it was easy to become disoriented. He was feeling more and more like Gnat, the child, again, and he was longing for the advice of his uncle, Dancing Rabbit. He wondered if he had been foolishly over-confident in making this trip alone. Maybe he wasn't ready. Maybe he would never be ready.

He stopped to catch his breath, and he recalled the story about Dancing Rabbit, alone, making his way home from a hostile, unfamiliar land somewhere to the far west, and he was ashamed of himself for his fear. He moved ahead.

Then he saw the clearing and in another few steps the village. He had figured his directions right after all. With a sigh of relief and a slightly lighter step, he headed for the village. When he saw them, it was too late, for they had seen him too. He stood for a moment unable to react except with wide eyes and an open mouth. The man before him was unlike any he had ever seen before.

His legs, torso and arms were covered in clothing, clothing that was strange to Carrier's eyes. The big hands were hairy, but Carrier could see that underneath the hair the skin was almost white. But the real horror was the face. It was an angry face, and like the hands, nearly white, but with a strange red-dish hue seemingly showing through the skin. The lower half of the face was covered with hair, and the hair on the head was long and shaggy. The effect was that all the face Carrier could see was eyes and a little ruddy skin around them.

And the expression on the face was surprise followed by a ferocious rage. The man shouted something. Carrier couldn't tell if he was shouting at him or at the other strangers, for the man kept looking at him. Carrier stood still, unable to react, frozen in place by astonishment and fear and, yes, curiosity.

Then the man stepped boldly and menacingly toward him.

He spoke again, his words unfamiliar and harsh, and as he moved, he reached for the handle of a long knife that dangled from a belt around his waist.

Carrier heard his own shout of fear, and it surprised him and startled him out of his trance. He turned to run. He heard the sounds behind him of the strange man shouting and crashing through the forest in pursuit. He thought he heard the sounds of others joining in the chase. He ran. He ran as hard as he could run.

His direction was determined by the easiest path he could find through the thick forest. He ran, dodging trees, low-hanging branches, tangled undergrowth too thick to run through. He ran leaping over obstacles in his path. He ran until he thought that his heart would burst inside his chest and his lungs would split open. He ran until he could no longer feel the tiredness or the pain in his legs. His numb legs seemed to be flying underneath him with some power and determination of their own.

At last he stopped and leaned against a tree trunk panting, gasping for breath, and there was no sound of pursuit behind him. No more crashing through the brush, no more clanking, no more strange, harsh voices shouting. He wondered how long he had kept running after the chasers had given up. Again he felt foolish and more than a little cowardly. Suddenly he felt a surging animosity toward the strangers who had caused him to react in such an unmanly way.

He started walking. He had no idea where he was going. He knew that there must be other villages of the Timucua people in the area, but the village which was now occupied by the ugly strangers was the only one he and his uncle had ever visited. They had never gone farther south than that. They had never ventured farther inland from the southwestern coastline.

He walked until his breathing was almost regular again, and then he sat down to rest. He realized that he was terribly hungry and thirsty. His mouth and throat felt dry and gritty and raspy, and he began to feel the pain in the muscles of his legs. He leaned back heavily against the trunk of an old, large tree, and, trying to ignore his discomforts, he began to assess his situation.

He was alone. He knew not where he was or where he was going. He had abandoned his bundle of wares, and it was likely, he decided, with the strangers in that vicinity, that they would discover the hiding place and confiscate the goods. At any rate, he knew that he would not go back through that area to retrieve the pack.

His bow and arrows, his blowgun and darts were all attached to the lost bundle. A flint knife was hanging from his belt. He had no other weapon. He was nearly naked, having packed away his shirts and leggings for the walk along the stretch of beach.

Well, the trip was a failure. That much was certain. His new goal was to simply get out of this country alive and to get back home. But he could not just start walking north again. He had to find food, and he would have to get himself resupplied for a long trip. Under the circumstances, the Timucuas would probably give him what he would need for that journey. So his immediate, short-term goal became to locate another Timucua village.

He got up and looked around himself, trying to decide upon a direction for his search. He was completely lost. He was even a little afraid that he might blunder stupidly right back into the hands of the strangers at the village which they occupied. The forest was thick, and overhead was a roof of heavily leafed branches which nearly blocked out any view of the sun.

He kept searching the canopy above until he managed to determine the location of the sun in the sky. It was going down in the west. West would lead him back to the beach. He did not want to go there. He walked east, deeper into the forest.

M. J.

Seven

CARRIER THOUGHT that he heard something behind him moving through the forest, traveling in his
own trail, following him. The noise was faint, so he did not
believe that it was the hairy-faced strangers again searching
for him. He stopped to listen more carefully, and he could
clearly discern a slight rustling of the forest floor. Someone or
something was coming up behind him. It was probably a man
of some kind. What animal would track a man like that? He
grasped the handle of the flint knife there at his waist, and he
noted that his palm was sweating. He waited pressed tight
against the trunk of a tall tree for what seemed like a long
time. No one came into view, but the rustling became a bit
louder, closer. He slowly pulled the knife loose and held it
ready.

He could tell from the noise of the footsteps, the legs
brushing through the tangle on the ground, that whoever or
whatever was coming was just about upon him. His heart
thumped hard in his chest. He raised the knife and jumped out

from behind his cover ready to do battle, and he found himself face to face with another man, not one of the strangers. Both men yelled almost simultaneously. Carrier dropped his knife in his surprise and fright. He bent to retrieve it.

"Don't strike," said the other, speaking in the trade language. "I'm not your enemy."

Carrier straightened up, his knife in hand again. He looked at the other with suspicion in his eyes.

"You're not a Timucua," he said.

"No. Nor are you."

"Who are you?" said Carrier.

"I'm called He-Fights-with-Alligators. I'm a Calusa, from south of here. I just escaped from the Españols."

The last word spoken by He-Fights-with-Alligators was totally unintelligible to Carrier. Even the sounds of the word were strange to his ears.

"From whom?" he asked.

"From the white men. The hairy-faced strangers. I was their captive."

"They were chasing me," said Carrier.

"I know. When they ran after you, I ran too. That's how I got away from them. May I know your name?"

"I'm Carrier, a trader from the Chilokis to the north of here. I was going to that village back there to trade. Then I saw those—white men."

"Where are you going now?"

"I don't know," said Carrier. "I don't know this country. I have only been to the one village in the past. There must be some more Timucua villages around here somewhere."

"There are. I know where to go. Will you go along with me?"

"Yes," said Carrier. "Let's go together."

He wasn't at all sure that he could trust this man. If his story was true, then he certainly should be trustworthy. But if he was working with those men, then he could be leading Carrier into a trap. But what choice did Carrier have? He was lost. This man was familiar with the country. He would go along with He-Fights-with-Alligators, but he would watch him carefully until he was able to make up his mind about the man.

"Lead the way," he said.

He-Fights-with-Alligators walked past Carrier. He kept walking without looking back. Carrier fell in step behind. They walked on for a good while in silence, and even though Carrier had not yet decided whether or not the Calusa was to be trusted, it did feel good to have some company again. Then they came to a small clearing in the forest beside where a fresh stream ran. The Calusa stopped and turned back to face Carrier.

"We should camp here for the night," he said. "The village isn't far from here, but if we keep going, it will be dark before we get there. With enemies in this country, I think it would be wise of us to try to arrive in the daylight."

"Yes," said Carrier. "I think you're right about that."

They built a small fire and scooped up piles of leaves to make soft places to sleep. They drank fresh water from the stream. Carrier's stomach was growling loud protests of hunger, but he said nothing about it. He would just have to wait, he decided, for even if they wanted to hunt for meat, Carrier had only his knife. The Calusa had no weapons.

But He-Fights-with-Alligators knelt down beside the stream and began digging with his fingers in the soft ground, pulling up certain plants by their roots. Carrier watched until the Calusa had a pile of the plants there beside him. Then He-Fights-with-Alligators picked up one of the plants and showed Carrier its large root.

"This is good to eat," he said. He dipped the root in the

running water and washed off the dirt. Then he took a bite of it and began to chew. He handed another plant to Carrier, who knelt down beside the water to imitate his new companion.

The roots were surprisingly good, and Carrier ate enough of them to appease his hunger. Then he stretched out on his bed of leaves. He groaned as he felt the pains of the day's activities in his muscles and bones and on his much abused skin.

"What did you say these strangers call themselves?" he asked.

"In their language, Español," said the Calusa. "They come from a place far across the water which they call España."

Carrier opened his mouth and said, hesitantly, *"Asquani?"*

"They have established themselves on an island to the south of us where they've enslaved all of the native population. But they always need more slaves, so they look up here. They also want gold. They're crazy for gold. They do anything to get it."

"How long were you with these—*'squanis?"*

He-Fights-with-Alligators stared at the small fire for a long moment as if he were looking for something in there.

"A long time," he said. "I don't know. Maybe a year. Maybe longer. I learned their language, and for that reason they took me with them to be their interpreter."

Carrier suddenly felt compassion for this Calusa, and he just as suddenly realized that he not only trusted but liked the man.

"I'm glad you escaped from them," he said. "I'm glad that my appearance there gave you the opportunity to run away."

The Calusa laughed unexpectedly and lay back on his own bed of leaves to stretch.

"I am, too, Carrier, my new friend," he said. "I'm glad you came along when you did."

They found the Timucua village early the next morning. After an initial burst of excitement followed by formal introductions, things settled down, and the two outsiders found themselves surrounded by a small group of questioners led by the chief of the village, a man called Big Mouth. Also in the group were Potmaker and her brother, Tree Frog. Carrier knew Tree Frog from previous trading trips, but he would not have recognized Potmaker. She had been but a girl when last he visited the Timucuan. Now he looked at her and saw a beautiful young woman.

Like most of the other women, Potmaker wore only a short skirt made of hanging moss. Her shining black hair reached as far down behind her as did the skirt. But Carrier didn't have the time and leisure to stare at Potmaker and dream. It was a time of crisis, and there were many questions being asked. Big Mouth pointed his chin at Carrier.

"You say you came to trade," he said. "Where are your goods?"

"When I saw the big boats in the water," said Carrier, "I took my pack off my back and hid it at the edge of the forest. I was afraid that I might meet those strangers and have to run from them or fight, and my pack was too much of a burden."

"And you did meet them?"

"Yes. I went through the forest to try to avoid them, but when I got to the village, they were there already. They saw me, and they chased me."

"And where did you meet this one," said Big Mouth, gesturing with his head toward the Calusa.

"He came up behind me in the forest."

"When the white men chased him," said He-Fights-with-Alligators, "I ran. I was their captive until then."

"He's the one who talked to us from the boats," said Potmaker.

"Yes," said the Calusa. "I've been a captive of the Españols for a long time. I learned their language, so they brought me here as interpreter."

"He warned us to run away from the strangers," said Tree Frog.

"I was speaking your language, so my captors couldn't understand the words. They thought I was saying what they told me to say. They know none of our languages. Only their own. Their Español."

"Tell us about these men," said Big Mouth.

"They come from a faraway land," said the Calusa. "The only way between our land and theirs is over the water, and they come in their big boats. Their ruler lives back there in their home, and so they are far away from him. They do as they please and fight among themselves.

"When they come to a land for the first time, they claim that they own it, that their ruler owns it, and everything and everybody on that land. They claim it for themselves. This land of ours, the Calusas, the Timucuas and the Apalachees to the north, the Españols have claimed, and they call it Florida. They call us, all of us, Timucuas, Apalachees, Calusas, Chilokis, all of us, they call Indios.

"The man in charge of the two boats here now is named in his language Francisco de Garay."

Big Mouth tried to repeat the name but could not. He brushed it aside as something of little or no importance.

"What does this man want here?" he said.

"All of the white men want gold and slaves, but one of them came here earlier with a tale about a spring, drinking the water of which will prevent one from growing old. They also look for that."

"Is there such a spring?" asked Big Mouth.

"I don't believe that there is," said He-Fights-with-Alligators. "But the Españols believe that everything they want is here somewhere for them to take. Gold makes them rich. They want all of it they can take. Slaves do all their work, so they always want more slaves. And they do not want to grow old and die."

"Everyone grows old," said Big Mouth. "Everyone dies. These men sound like fools."

"They are fools, I think," said the Calusa, "but they are very dangerous fools."

"Tell me about their weapons," said Big Mouth.

"From metals which they dig out of the earth, they make a very hard substance which they call steel. From that steel they make their knives and their breastplates and their shields. They have short bows which they call crossbows. They shoot short arrows, but they shoot them far and fast and hard. And they have other weapons which they call guns. Some of them are big and on wheels. Some are small to be carried in their arms. They put a black powder in the guns, and then they put bits of metal. They make a spark, and the black powder ignites and explodes. That makes the metal fly through the air. These guns are very dangerous, but they can only shoot them one time. Then they have to load them all over again."

Big Mouth sat as if in deep thought for a long silence. Then he nodded toward Potmaker.

"What are these men doing in this woman's village, do you think?"

"I heard them say they were going to establish their own town there. They mean to stay."

Big Mouth's face grew dark and somber, and he stood up, towering over all those around him who remained seated. The full feathered cloak which had concealed his seated figure fell open to reveal his muscular body, totally covered with tattoos declaring his great exploits in war.

"We will not allow that," he said. "These men from across the water cannot live here in our land. We will send them a message telling them so. If they refuse to leave after we have warned them, then we will attack and drive them out or kill them."

"I would like to help you with this," said He-Fights-with-Alligators.

"And I," said Carrier.

"You're our guests here," said Big Mouth. "Stay as long as you like. If it comes to a fight, fight with us if you like."

The chief turned to walk back to his own house, and the group began to break apart. Carrier and his new Calusa friend stayed. Tree Frog and his sister were still there, too. Potmaker took a step toward Carrier.

"I'm sorry that your visit to us came at such a time," she said. "I'd like to be able to say that I'm glad to see you again. I'd like to be able to welcome you to my own village and offer you a meal and a place to sleep. Now that's not my place, for I, too, am a guest in this town."

"It's a bad time," said Carrier, "but still I'm glad to see you. And if I can be of help, that too will please me."

Eight

THE GUESTS OF THE VILLAGE all slept in the large townhouse, the men on one side and the women on the other. A small fire was left burning in the middle of the room. Carrier lay down with a disarray of thoughts racing through his mind. He could not remember ever having been more tired before in his life, yet he wondered if the thoughts would allow him to sleep.

He thought about the beautiful Timucua woman known as Potmaker. As far as he could tell, she was unmarried and not spoken for. He longed to know her better. He longed—even though he told himself the thought was foolish for he did not even really know her—he longed to take her home with him as his wife.

Lying in the darkness of the townhouse, knowing that she was there under the same roof, he tried to recall every detail of her physical appearance, and he tried to recall her voice. He longed to feel her touch.

But these thoughts, which were both pleasant and painful,

struggled for prominence in his mind with others, thoughts of the horrible strangers, images of their terrible appearance, vague remembrances of their harsh voices and strange-sounding language, and the tales he had heard from the Apalachee of their incredible brutality.

And then there was the worry, the uncertainty, the anticipation of what the next few days might bring. Big Mouth was going to send a warning to the white men. Carrier doubted that the strangers would heed the warning. That meant there would be a battle. If so, Carrier meant to take part. He had already said so in front of many people. Besides, the *Ani-'squani* had startled him, caused him to yell out in fright and run like a coward. He felt a need to show them that he was no coward. He was a man of the Real People, *Ani-yunwi-ya*.

He wondered if the Timucuas would conduct a ceremony in preparation for war before attacking the occupied village. He hoped so, for the Real People, his own people, never went into battle without conducting the proper ceremonies if they had a choice. Of course, if some enemy came upon them unexpectedly, they had no choice.

That thought suggested to him another worry. What, he asked himself, if the white men found this village and attacked it before Big Mouth was ready? They would have a certain amount of time to prepare to defend themselves, for the sentries that Big Mouth had put out would see and hear the enemy coming. But that would not give them time to perform the ceremonies. He wondered if he should ask Big Mouth about that.

The morning brought an answer to Carrier's question without his having to ask it. A crier went all around the village with the announcement. The people were to prepare to do battle, just in case the strangers refused to heed the warning which was to be issued by Big Mouth. Those who intended to take part in the battle, men or women, were to abstain from all food beginning immediately. They would fast for four days. Each night there would be dancing. The conjurers would begin right away making medicine for victory. Then Big Mouth sent for He-Fights-with-Alligators.

"You alone can speak to these men," said the chief. "You will have to carry the message. Are you willing to do that for us?"

"I've said that I would help you," said the Calusa. "I'll take the message, but I'd like to take some men with me. Those Españols will try to take me captive again."

"Take whomever you like," said Big Mouth, "but go at once."

He-Fights-with-Alligators went back to the townhouse. Carrier was still there, talking with Tree Frog and Potmaker. The Calusa joined them.

"I'm going now to take Big Mouth's message to the white men," he said. "But I need to find some men to go with me. I don't want to be captured again."

"I'll go," said Carrier.

"And I," said Tree Frog. "I'm not afraid of those men."

When the three men left the village, they were armed with long bows and arrows, knives and warclubs supplied for them by their hosts. They started west on the trail that ran directly between the two villages. They walked along for a short while in silence. Then the Calusa spoke.

"When we get there," he said, "the Españols will try to capture us or kill us."

"When we bring a message?" said Carrier.

"Yes. They have no sense of honor."

"Then wait," said Tree Frog. "I know a trail through the forest that will bring us to the top of a hill outside of my village. We can get there without anyone seeing us. Then you can shout the message down at them. They'll hear you, and if they try to catch us, we'll be able to get away from them easily."

"Good," said the Calusa. "You lead the way then."

Tree Frog moved out ahead, and the other two followed. In a little while, he led them into the forest on a trail that was barely perceptible from the main path. By midday they had reached the hilltop that was their destination, and they were looking down on the occupied village. He-Fights-with-Alligators took a deep breath and stepped forward.

"Españols," he shouted. "Don Francisco de Garay. It is I. The one you call Paco. But I am not Paco. I am He-Fights-with-Alligators of the Calusa People. Listen to me. I bring a message from Big Mouth, chief of the next town of Timucua People."

Neither Carrier nor Tree Frog could understand anything of what the Calusa was saying, for he was speaking in the language of the strangers. Nor, of course, did they understand the angry shout that came from the village below in response to what the Calusa had said.

"Big Mouth says that you are to leave this land," the Calusa continued. "Go now and go in peace. If you refuse, you will be attacked and wiped out. That is the message from Big Mouth."

Another shout came from below, and one of the white men raised a weapon to his shoulder. He-Fights-with-Alligators shouted and turned at the same time.

"Run," he said. "They are coming after us."

As the three messengers ran down the back side of the hill, they heard a loud explosion from behind them. They raced back into the forest and started back on the same trail they had used before. Soon the Calusa stopped them.

"Wait," he said. He listened for a moment. "They're not following us," he added. "You two go back and tell Big Mouth that I delivered his message. I'm going back to that hilltop to watch and listen. When I learn anything, I'll return to the village."

"You want to stay here alone?" said Carrier.

"It's best alone. I'll hide and watch and listen. They won't see me or hear me. Go on now."

Carrier and Tree Frog hesitated only a moment, then ran ahead. Carrier didn't feel good about leaving the Calusa alone, but he didn't know what else to do. Perhaps it made sense that one man alone would be better off. He hoped so. He didn't want anything to happen to his new friend.

Back at Big Mouth's town, Carrier and Tree Frog reported to the chief. They told him that his message had been delivered and that the Calusa had stayed behind to spy on the strangers. Then they returned to the townhouse. There they found many of the Timucua men painting themselves in preparation for the evening dance. Carrier decided that he would watch this first night to see if he could learn the Timucua ways. If he could figure it out easily enough, he would take part the next three nights.

He was sitting watching the men when Potmaker approached him.

"My brother said that the Calusa stayed to watch our village," she said.

"Yes," said Carrier, "to see if he could overhear something about the intentions of the strangers."

"Will he be all right alone?"

"I hope so. He said that it was safer for just one. It's easier to hide."

"He's probably right about that. Will you dance tonight with us?"

"I don't know your ways," he said. "I'll watch tonight. Maybe I'll dance tomorrow."

She sat down beside him, and he tried to keep his eyes from staring at her long and lovely legs.

"Do you think," he said, "that it would be all right if I were to carve myself a mask?"

"What kind of mask?" she asked.

"At home, before going to war, very often a man will carve a mask. On the forehead of the mask there will be a rattlesnake coiled. It shows that the wearer is not afraid—of anything."

"Would you wear this mask when you dance?"

"Yes."

"I think it would be all right."

"Then in the morning, I'll start to make my mask."

They sat there on the bench in the townhouse side by side for a while longer in awkward silence. Then she shifted her weight as if to rise, as if to leave. He stopped her with a word.

"Potmaker," he said.

She settled back and glanced at him for an instant, then looked back at the ground between her feet.

"Yes?"

"What is the custom among your people—when a man wants to marry a woman?"

"He asks the woman if she likes him," she said.

"And if she does?"

"Then the two of them go together to her parents and tell them what they want to do. If the parents don't object, they marry. They build a new house and move into it."

"That's all?"

"Yes. That's all."

She waited for him to say more, but he didn't. Not on the subject of marriage.

"I wonder if the white men will attack us here before we're ready," he said.

Tree Frog ran into the townhouse just at that moment.

"Come on outside," he said. "They're ready to begin."

As he had planned, Carrier watched. Most of the young Timucua men danced, Tree Frog among them. Those whose bodies were already covered with tattoos did not bother to paint themselves. The permanent designs already proclaimed all their exploits. Others were painted.

Hair was pulled up on top of heads and tied into topknots, some of which were adorned with several arrows pushed through. Others were decorated with the colorful feathers of tropical birds. The men wore only breechclouts and carried symbolic warclubs carved from wood and painted red. The dance went from east to north to west to south around the fire in the center of the cleared grounds in front of the townhouse. The songs were unfamiliar to Carrier, but the dances, though different in some details, were generally like those of his own people. He decided that he would dance the next three nights with the Timucuas.

The next morning, Carrier started to make his mask. A man named Panther showed him where he could get the wood and loaned him the necessary tools. Carrier carved a face with a stern expression. Its eyebrows were made of a single line with the ends of the line curving upward. The eyeholes were small and close-set. The lips were tight and turned down, and deep lines ran from the nostrils of the large nose down to each side of the mouth.

The rest of the face was smooth with no more attention

paid to detail, but on the front of the head was carved a coiled rattlesnake, the rattles, the patterns on the back, even the face painstakingly finished. The whole mask was then painted red, and fox fur was attached to the sides of the face just where the ears might have been. Carrier finished the mask by drilling a hole in each side and attaching a rawhide thong with which to tie it in place over his own face. Then he sat back and studied his handiwork. It was not as good as Doya might have done, but it would certainly serve his purpose. He was satisfied. He was proud.

That night, Carrier danced with the Timucuas. He danced wearing the mask with the rattlesnake on its head. He felt bold. In spite of what had happened when he first encountered the white men, he was here publicly declaring his bravery. The rattlesnake said that he had no fear. He was not afraid of the *Ani-'squani*. He was not afraid of anything. No man bold enough to display on his own head *ujonati* could have any fear.

He danced, and as he danced his fury increased, his determination to help his friends drive the strangers from their land grew, his confidence in his own warrior's skills expanded. He knew that he would be successful. He knew that he and his friends would taste victory. He felt good.

Nine

WHEN CARRIER WOKE UP on the morning of the third day of the preparations, he no longer felt the hunger of the fast. He felt only exhilaration. He was light-headed. He was anxious for the battle. He looked forward eagerly to the dancing that would take place again that night, to boasting again that he felt no fear.

He and the other men who were planning to go to battle had been confined to the townhouse for the preparations, and the women who had previously been guests in there had been moved out. There was to be no more contact between men and women, not until after the battle and after the purification rites which would follow it. These practices were all familiar to Carrier, and he accepted them without question. It was the way these things were done.

Carrier figured that it must be about midday. The men in the townhouse were lounging about, smoking their pipes, talking of the upcoming fight with the strangers, when Big Mouth came in with the Calusa, He-Fights-with-Alligators. Everyone looked to the newcomers.

"The strangers are coming to attack us," said Big Mouth. "We won't have time to finish the ceremonies. The first two days will have to be enough. Right now, the Big Conjurer is busy talking to the spirits to make things right."

"When are the hairy faces coming?" asked one of the men.

Big Mouth turned toward the Calusa.

"They are on their way now," said He-Fights-with-Alligators.

"Get your weapons," instructed Big Mouth. "We will not wait for them to attack us here in our homes. We will meet them on the trail."

Carrier stood in confusion, knowing that something of importance was being discussed but not understanding the Timucua speech. He turned toward Tree Frog, who then translated it all for him.

"It's not good," said Tree Frog.

"But it will have to do," said Carrier. "We can't sit here and let them attack us and the whole village."

"No. We can't."

"Do you know the conjurer of this town?"

"I know of him," said Tree Frog. "He's said to be very powerful."

"Then maybe all will be well," said Carrier. "Maybe he can make it all right."

"Perhaps," said Tree Frog. "Perhaps. Well, let's get our weapons. They'll leave us behind."

Carrier was not too surprised to see that about a dozen women had joined the men who were planning to meet the strangers to do battle. That sometimes happened at home among his own people. Women were not particularly encouraged to go into battle, but they were certainly not forbidden to do so if they made that decision. It was unusual, but it sometimes happened, and often the women proved to be ferocious fighters.

He was a little surprised, however, to see that Potmaker was among them. For some reason, he had not expected that. It made him proud of her, though. He liked her better than ever. Even so, a part of him wished that she had not chosen to go into this fight with the white, hairy-faced strangers. He would be concerned about her safety during the fight. He did not want anything bad to happen to Potmaker. Well, it was her decision, and there was nothing he could do about it. She would have to take care of herself. He would have to worry about his own safety and about defeating the enemy. She would be doing the same thing, as would all the others, men and women alike.

He was pleased to note that Big Mouth was going along as war leader. He had not known what to expect from the Timucua chief. Among his own people, following the reorganization of recent years, each town had two chiefs, one for war and one for peace. The peace chief was not allowed to go to war even if he should want to. Carrier had not been able to determine if there was any chief in this Timucua town other than Big Mouth. Perhaps the Timucua people had but one town chief.

They started walking single file down the trail toward the occupied village. If the Calusa's information was correct, they would encounter the enemy somewhere along the way. They had not gone far when Carrier noticed Big Mouth speaking to two men up at the front of the line. The two then ran into the forest, one on each side of the trail. The main group, following Big Mouth, who was still in the lead, continued straight ahead.

In a short while the two men reappeared, and Big Mouth halted the march. He held a short conversation with the two, then turned and spoke an order. Carrier gave Tree Frog, who was walking just behind him, a questioning look.

"He said for us to go into the forest," said Tree Frog, "and wait. The white men are not far from us now. Some of us are to go right and some left, and when the white men are well in between us, we are to start shooting arrows."

The warriors, male and female, were already stepping off the trail and into the edge of the forest. Soon the trail appeared to be deserted. Carrier squatted behind some brush close to the trail's edge. A large tree stood just to his right. His heart pounded with anticipation. His breaths were short and fast, and he thought that they were loud enough to be heard by the men on either side of him.

Remember to miss the hard shirts, he told himself. Arrows cannot penetrate them. Aim for the places where the skin shows or where the clothing is soft.

The wait seemed long, too long. Carrier began to wonder if the two scouts had been right. Perhaps the white men had tricked them somehow. They should be here already, he thought. Where are they? Why are they not here?

And then he heard them. The first sound to reach his ears was the loud clanking of metal. Then came the noise of the hoofs of the large animals. He heard no voices. The men were riding along in silence, he guessed. That made good sense to him. They were planning an attack. Well, they were about to get a big surprise. Imaginary images of the carnage to come flickered through his mind. His palms were wet with sweat.

The enemy came closer, and the noises became louder and clearer and more terrifying. Behind the cover of the tree trunk, Carrier nocked an arrow in the long Timucua bow and waited. Then he saw the first 'squani, and a terrible fright went through his body. It was almost as bad as when he had seen the other one, the one that had surprised him and made him run like a child. Riding on the back of the great animal, the man seemed almost a monster. Man and animal were covered by pieces of the hard metal, and nothing showed of the man's face but a little skin around the eyes. The bottom part of the face was covered with hair, and a hard metal hat was on his head. In his right arm, he carried a long lance.

The other riders were close behind him. They rode single file. The trail was too narrow for them to do otherwise. Carrier was just about to draw the long bow when an arrow from the other side of the trail hit the second mounted man in the neck. The man screamed in pain as blood gushed out from the wound.

Then everything seemed to happen at once. Arrows flew from both sides of the trail. Most of them seemed to shatter on or bounce off the hard shirts and shields. There was screaming and shouting from both sides, and the big animals added their own eerie screams to the noise.

There was no command, there had been no prearranged understanding, but all of a sudden, the Timucuas and their allies seemed to all rush out from their cover to chop and hack at the white men and the big animals with their warclubs. Carrier saw a man knocked down by one of the beasts. He did not see what happened to the man after that. He was too busy fighting his own fight.

He rushed at the big *'squani* at the head of the column. The man tried to swing his lance into play, but it was too long to maneuver there in the narrow trail. He dropped it and reached for the long knife at his side. Carrier swung his warclub as hard as he could, and he managed to strike the man's right elbow. As the man shrieked in pain and anger, the arm dropped useless to his side. He struggled to pull out the long knife with his left arm, but Carrier kept swinging.

The man leaned farther and farther to his left to avoid the

blows. Then he fell off his animal's back and landed heavily on the ground. For a moment Carrier was confused and hesitant. The nervous, stamping beast was between him and his foe. He started to go around in front of the animal, but its great head was shaking and bobbing up and down. Its eyes were wild, and it made hideous noises as strings of froth dangled and swung from its mouth.

Carrier turned to go around behind, but the next man in line was close behind, and the fight going on back there was deadly. To go that way, he would have to make his way between the front of one beast and the back of another, and both were stamping around dangerously. Suddenly recklessly bold, Carrier dropped to his hands and knees and scrambled beneath the beast's belly to pounce upon the fallen *'squani*. The man was lying on his back, struggling to rise. Carrier straddled the fallen man's torso and raised his own warclub high. The man growled like a wounded animal and clawed at Carrier's eyes with his left hand, but Carrier brought the warclub down, smashing the side of the man's face. He struck again and again until he knew that the man was dead. The loose animal ran wildly ahead.

Carrier stood and looked back on the rest of the battle. He saw a Timucua struggling with a man still on the back of his beast, reaching up, trying to pull his enemy down. The man raised a foot and shoved the Timucua back, causing him to fall. Then he lifted his shooting tube and aimed it at the fallen Timucua. The tube made a loud noise, like thunder, and spat fire, and the Timucua yelled as his chest was torn open by the flying bits of metal.

Carrier ran to the side of the trail and picked up the long bow he had abandoned there. He fitted an arrow to the string and drew back the powerful Timucua bow, taking quick aim. He released the arrow, and it flew straight, driving itself into the right eye of the man with the shooting tube. The man screamed and fell backward off his animal to land hard on the back of his head and his shoulders with a thud and a clank. His body clattered as it settled and he died.

Carrier saw He-Fights-with-Alligators drag a man off the back of an animal and slice his throat with a knife. And he saw one of the strangers swing his long knife and nearly slice the head off Big Mouth, the Timucua chief. He did not see Potmaker, and he wondered about her. He wondered where she was and how she was doing.

Then, amazingly clear over the din of battle, a white man's voice rang out, and all of the big animals with men on their backs turned around in the trail and began racing back toward the occupied village. A few Timucuas flung their warclubs or shot arrows after them. Many had already scattered back into the forest.

Carrier looked around. The Calusa was still standing there. So was Tree Frog. There were a few others. One man walked over to stand beside the body of the fallen Big Mouth. He said a few words in the Timucua language, which Carrier, of course, could not understand. He looked toward Tree Frog.

"He said that we're without a leader," said Tree Frog, using the trade language for Carrier's benefit. "We'll have to go back to the village to select someone else."

"Eight of us are killed," said He-Fights-with-Alligators.

"Twelve of the strangers," said Tree Frog.

"Some of the strangers who rode away were hurt," said the Calusa.

"And some of us," added Tree Frog. "We don't know either who we may yet find in the forest, hurt or dead."

The Timucua spoke again, and again Tree Frog interpreted for Carrier.

"Let's go back to the village," he said, "and get some others to help us carry back our dead. We'll also find out who has survived and whether or not we need to search for more bodies in the forest."

"You go ahead with that," said He-Fights-with-Alligators. "I'm going back through the woods to spy on the Españols again. I'll try to find out how badly we hurt them and what they intend to do next."

"Come back and let us know as soon as you find out anything," said the Timucua.

"Yes. Of course I will."

Once more, the Calusa, the former slave of the people he called Españols, disappeared into the forest. Carrier looked at Tree Frog. Both men looked toward the other Timucua standing there. Carrier wanted to look around for Potmaker. He wanted to ask if anyone had seen her. He hoped that she had escaped and made her way back to the village. The Timucua spoke, and Tree Frog translated for Carrier.

"Let's take up the body of our fallen chief and go back to the village."

Carrier nodded in agreement.

"Yes," he said. "We've delayed too long already, I think."

Ten

THEY REPORTED THE RESULTS of the battle to the people back at the village, and they got some help to bring back the rest of the bodies. Then there was wailing for the dead, and there were preparations for the funerals. All of this had to take place while those who had taken part in the battle were being purified, for they had shed blood, and they had taken lives.

But they were in a dangerous situation, a deadly one, one that called for extreme measures, and even though the things of the spirit must necessarily be attended to, there were other things, worldly things, that also had to be done. Tree Frog, by force of his personality, took the lead in the absence of a town chief.

"I think that runners should go to all the Timucua villages," he said. "Everyone who is able and willing to fight these white men should come here. They should come as soon as possible."

"But we killed more of them than they of us," said one. "Perhaps they'll go away now."

"Yes," said another. "We showed them that Timucuas are not so easy to kill."

"Timucuas will never be their slaves."

"They ran from us like cowards, ran away on their big animals."

"Maybe you're right," said Tree Frog. "I hope you are. But how many of them did we meet in battle?"

There was a brief pause and some low muttering. Then one of the men ventured an answer to Tree Frog's question.

"I think there were maybe twenty of them," he said. "And we killed twelve. The other eight ran away."

"Two big boats came," said Tree Frog. "How many strangers on each boat?"

"The Calusa who had been with them said one hundred."

"One hundred on each boat?"

"Yes."

"Then out of two hundred men, they sent only twenty to attack this village here."

"Well, yes."

"Then I guess that they didn't think that we could fight. They thought it would be an easy battle to win. Now they found out that we can fight, so the next time they come, I think, they'll send more. I think we'd better be ready for them to come back. I think that we had better be ready for as many as one hundred. Maybe more. I think if we can get enough people together here before they attack us again, I think we should attack them first—back at my village, at the village there where they are staying."

At last they decided to follow Tree Frog's advice, and runners went out to all of the other Timucua villages, asking them to send all their warriors for a big gathering to drive out or wipe out the strangers.

"Where is the Calusa?" someone asked. "He should go ask his people to join us in this fight."

"We don't need the Calusas," said another.

"The Calusa has gone back to spy on the white men," said Tree Frog. "He understands their language, and maybe he'll overhear something. When he learns anything, he'll be back here to let us know."

While all this was going on, Carrier was looking over the crowd, searching in vain for some sign of Potmaker. At last the meeting broke up, and the people went about their business. Carrier approached Tree Frog.

"I haven't seen your sister," he said.

"Nor have I," said Tree Frog.

"Do you think she made it back here all right?"

"I don't think so. She would have been here with the others."

"What should we do?" said Carrier. "She might be in trouble somewhere."

"Let's you and I go back and search the woods again around the battle site."

Tree Frog didn't say what they would be searching for, and Carrier didn't ask. Neither man wanted to admit aloud that they might be searching for a body. That was the worst possibility. She might be hurt too badly to get home on her own. Or she might have been captured by the white men.

No one in the village seemed to know anything about her. No one had seen her caught or killed or hurt. Carrier was frustrated by that lack of news, but he wasn't really surprised by it. The battle had been chaotic, furious beyond imagination. He had never seen anything like it before, had never dreamed that he would ever see anything like it. He was sure that the fight had the same effect on all the others who had taken part in it. Therefore, he did not find it difficult to understand that no one had seen what had happened to Potmaker. He nodded in response to Tree Frog's suggestion.

"Let's go then," he said.

They searched the woods around the battle site until the sun was low in the western sky, and then they went slowly and dejectedly back to the village. They had seen no sign of Potmaker, nor did they find any other bodies of their own people. Everyone was accounted for except Potmaker. They did discover that the strangers had not bothered to return for the bodies of their own slain.

"What kind of men are these?" asked Carrier. "They let their dead lie on the ground neglected."

"I don't think they're real human beings," said Tree Frog. "They're some kind of animal that looks something like human beings. That's all."

It was the middle of the next day when He-Fights-with-Alligators returned to the village. A number of the people quickly gathered around him to hear what he might have to say. Tree Frog and Carrier were in front of the crowd.

"What are the white men doing?" said one.

"Are they going back to their boats? Are they leaving?"

"Are they coming back this way to attack us again?"

The Calusa held up a hand, and all grew quiet.

"They're not leaving," he said. "More of them have come in from the boats. They seem to be settling in the village to stay. I think they intend to make what they call a colony."

"What is that—that word you said?"

"It's a town one people make in the land of another people."

"Why do they want to do that?"

"They steal from the land: gold, furs, slaves. Then they

send those things back to their home. That's the way they get rich. The colony makes it easier for them to do that."

"So they're not going away," said Tree Frog.

"No," said He-Fights-with-Alligators. "I believe that they mean to stay right where they are. They won't go away unless they're driven away."

"Then let's drive them away," shouted one.

"Or kill them all," said another.

Then Tree Frog told the Calusa about the runners who had been sent out to gather the Timucua forces together in anticipation of another fight.

"We thought that you should go to your people and get them to help us," said one.

"I could do that, and I think that they would help," said the Calusa. "If you want me to go to them, I will. I've not seen my home for a long time."

During all this discussion, Carrier was lost, for all the talk was in the Timucua language, and the two men he relied on for translation were both involved in the exchange. Carrier didn't want to interrupt to ask what was going on. That would have been rude. He would wait until a more opportune time to ask Tree Frog or the Calusa to explain. But there was a pause following the Calusa's last statement, and in that pause, Tree Frog turned toward Carrier.

"What is it?" said Carrier, and Tree Frog gave him a brief translation of what had just occurred.

"If He-Fights-with-Alligators goes to his people," said Carrier, "who will spy on the white men? No one else can understand their language."

Continuing with the trade language, Tree Frog turned back to the Calusa.

"Do you hear what the white men are saying when you're watching them?" he asked.

"Not always. It's hard to get close enough. But sometimes I hear them."

"Then I think you need to stay here," said Tree Frog. "If we send someone else to talk to your people, will they listen?"

"Send our friend Carrier," said the Calusa. "I think they'll listen to him. Our own people, yours and mine, have sometimes fought with each other. My people know about the Chilokis and have sometimes traded with them. I think Carrier should go."

"Will you do this?" Tree Frog asked Carrier.

"Yes. I will."

Tree Frog then repeated all of that last conversation in the Timucua tongue for the other people standing around there. Then, "It's been decided," he said. The crowd dispersed, leaving Tree Frog, Carrier and He-Fights-with-Alligators standing there alone.

"Have you seen my sister?" asked Tree Frog.

The Calusa hesitated a moment, as if searching for the right words. Then he spoke bluntly.

"Yes," he said. "She's there. The Españols have her."

"We have to get her out of there," said Carrier, his voice betraying his desperation and his special concern.

"It would be a dangerous thing to attempt," said the Calusa. "The village is well guarded, and most of the Españols have left the big boats and moved into the village. Potmaker is being kept in the house where Francisco de Garay himself is staying, and he has extra guards around him all the time."

"And besides, you have a different mission now, my friend," said Tree Frog. "I know that you care about my sister. I've seen it. But don't worry. I care about her too. Perhaps as much as you do. While you're away, we'll see what we can do to get her out. I know you want to help, but it's more important just now that you go to the Calusas."

"Tree Frog is right, my friend," said He-Fights-with-Alligators. "You go to my people and convince them to join us here, and we'll do what we can to rescue Potmaker from the Españols."

There was nothing for Carrier to do but agree, though he did so reluctantly. He hated to think of Potmaker as a captive of the *Ani-'squani*, perhaps a slave. He hated to think of what they might do to her. He tried to push those unpleasant thoughts out of his mind, and he turned to the Calusa.

"I don't know your country," he said. "Can you tell me the way to go?"

"Yes, and whom to see when you get there. Come over here with me."

He-Fights-with-Alligators led Carrier to a spot where the ground was smooth and clear of growth. He drew in the dirt with a stick, showing the trails that wound through the forest going south. He told him how many days to walk before taking a turn, and he told him when he would reach the first Calusa town by this route.

"Will you remember this?" he asked.

"Yes," said Carrier. "I'll get there all right."

"When you walk into the village," said the Calusa, "identify yourself. Use the trade language. Many people there know it. Ask for Creeping Panther. No one else. He's the chief of the village, and he's my maternal uncle.

"Tell Creeping Panther that I'm alive. Tell him how we met. Then tell him what's happening here and why I stayed behind. Tell him that I sent you in my place and that I ask that he bring our warriors up here to join with the Timucuas to drive the Españols out of our land. Tell him all that, and he'll return with you. Do you remember all?"

"Yes," said Carrier. "I remember it all."

The Calusa sat back on his haunches and stared toward the south.

"It's been a long time," he said, "a very long time. They probably think that I'm dead. They'll be surprised to hear that I'm not only alive but free."

Then his brow wrinkled and a dark expression came over his face.

"Some may not be so pleased," he said. "I had a wife. She's probably found herself another man by now. And I had children. They wouldn't know me."

Carrier reached out and put a hand on his friend's shoulder.

"Don't worry," he said. "I feel sure that all will be well. I'll ask about your wife and children for you."

"No. I know you mean well, but don't ask. Don't talk to anyone except my uncle, and tell him only what I've said. No more. Will you do as I ask?"

Carrier looked at the Calusa for a brief moment. Then he looked away.

"Yes, my friend," he said. "I'll do exactly as you say."

M·J·

Eleven

AS CARRIER TRAVELED ALONE once again, this time in totally unfamiliar territory, farther south than he had ever gone before, he considered the problem of the *Ani 'squani*. He recalled that Tree Frog had suggested they might not really be human beings at all, and Carrier thought perhaps his Timucua friend was correct. He thought about all the monster stories he had been told all his life, and he tried to compare the images in his mind to the reality of the *Ani- 'squani*. These strangers, he concluded, seemed much more like the monsters than like human beings.

He considered, for example, the monster Untsaiyi, whose name was the imitation of the sound of something striking a sheet of metal, he who was also known as the Gambler. He was made of metal, probably copper or bronze, for in the old tale, when the little hard-shelled beetle struck him sharply on the forehead, making the sound *'chai*, the beetle's head was stained with green. And, so the story goes, it has been that way ever since.

The Gambler could change his shape at will, to become anything he wanted to be. He could take on the appearance of an old woman or an old man or some kind of animal—anything he chose. The squirrel chattering on a branch overhead, the snake slithering along the ground, the crow flying high in the sky, the waddling, lumbering bear, skunk, bat, anything one might come across might not be what it appeared to be at all. It might as easily be the Gambler.

He had invented the *gatayusti* game, the gambling game they played with the stone wheel and spear, and it was the all-consuming passion of his life. He tried to force everyone who passed his home to play the game with him, and he hated to lose, but when he did, he refused to pay his debts. He would bet everything he owned, up to and including his life, and if he lost that final game, he would run away.

And the Gambler could not die. The sons of Thunder, the two Little Thunders and Lightning, in the old story, acting on their father's advice, at last pinned the Gambler to the ocean floor to remain there until the end of the world.

Then there was U-tluh-da, the Spear-finger, who had the appearance of an ordinary old woman so long as she kept her one long sharp finger hidden under her shawl. But she had immense strength, and her skin was as hard as a rock. Her food was human livers, and she would entice children to her and then stick them through with her long finger and eat their livers.

She sang her song as she walked along alone through the woods, and if anyone happened to overhear, he would know that she was no ordinary old woman but the fearful and dreaded Spear-finger, the horrible killer of children and eater of livers, for this is what she sang.

> *Uwe-la-na-tsi-ga. Su sa sai.*
> *Uwe-la-na-tsi-ga. Su sa sai.*

Liver, I eat it. *Su sa sai.*
Liver, I eat it. *Su sa sai.*

Whenever they shot her with arrows, the arrows broke against her hard skin and fell useless at her feet. At last some men trapped her in a pitfall. They surrounded the hole and shot their arrows down at her, but the arrows broke as always, and she was trying to get out of the hole to get at them. She was furious, and her right fist was clenched, but the long, sharp right index finger stuck out menacingly.

Then Utsugi, the titmouse, sang a song to them, and the song sounded to the men like *unahu*, heart, and they thought that the little bird was telling them to shoot at her heart. So they did, but still the arrows broke and fell to the ground in pieces. Then they called Utsugi a liar, and they cut off its tongue, and it flew away.

Then Tsikilili, the chickadee, sang to them to get their attention, and it flew right down into the pit there with Spear-finger and lighted on her right fist, which was still tightly clenched. Spear-finger howled with rage and swung her arms about, and Tsikilili flew away, but the men had noticed, and they shot the right hand with several arrows, and Spear-finger shrieked and howled in pain and anger and fell down and died there in the pit, and they discovered then that she had kept her heart in that fist.

And he remembered the story of Nun-yunu-wi, Dressed-in-Stone. He looked like a harmless old man, but his skin was thick, solid stone. And he carried a walking stick that he would point occasionally, and then he would sniff its end. If he had pointed it toward where people were, he would be able to smell them on the end of the stick, and he would find them and kill them and eat them.

And if he came to a river, he could throw down his stick, and it would grow and stretch itself all the way across the river and become a bridge. Then Dressed-in-Stone would walk across the bridge to the other side, and the bridge would become a walking stick again, and he would pick it up and continue along his path.

There was only one thing that could harm Dressed-in-Stone, and that was the sight of a woman during her time of the month. One day as Dressed-in-Stone was walking toward a village of the Real People, some hunters spotted him and ran back to tell the others that he was coming their way. Quickly they asked around the village, and they found seven women who were in that condition. They placed these seven women, naked, along the path that led to the village.

At the sight of the first woman, Dressed-in-Stone covered his eyes and groaned out loud.

"What are you doing out in that state?" he said, but he walked on by her. Then he came to the second one.

"Oh," he said. "You should be hidden away somewhere." He walked on farther and came to the third woman, and he gagged and hurried past. Then he saw the fourth one, and he howled in pain. At the sight of the fifth, he staggered and stumbled. He crawled groaning alongside the sixth one, and when he came finally to the seventh and last of the bleeding women, he rolled over on his back gasping for breath.

Then the men came running, and they drove seven sourwood stakes through his body, pinning him to the ground, and they piled great logs over him and set fire to them. But before the flames reached him, before he died, Dressed-in-Stone gave to the Real People all the knowledge of healing plants, and he sang to them all of the hunting songs.

The *Ani-'squani* reminded Carrier of these monsters. They were frightful, and they were killers. He did not know whether the *Ani-'squani* ate people or not, but they did wear clothing that, like the stone coats of the monsters, would shatter arrows on impact. He wondered then if he and his friends did manage to kill the invaders, if they would learn something valuable from them at last, the way the Real People had learned from Dressed-in-Stone.

And there was Flint, whose name was the same as the material of which he was made. According to the tale, Flint had killed many animals and so was greatly feared by them. But flint is not like other rocks. It splits and shatters more easily, and for the benefit of all the animals, Rabbit shattered Flint with a mallet, scattering pieces of flint all over. Perhaps, thought Carrier, there was a way to shatter these white men into millions of pieces.

The other thing that occupied the mind of Carrier as he traveled was the fate of Potmaker. He felt bad about leaving her in the hands of the enemy, especially such a horrible enemy as the white men were, even though his mission was an especially important one, even though Potmaker's own brother had assured Carrier that he would do everything he could to rescue his sister and bring her back home safely. Carrier hoped for the best, yet he imagined the worst.

Well, there was nothing for it, he told himself, but to locate Creeping Panther, accomplish his mission and get back to the Timucuas as quickly as possible. Then, if Potmaker was still a captive, he could try to save her himself.

He hurried toward his destination, and he realized that he was in danger of wearing himself out, running himself down. He had to force himself to adopt a slower pace, one that could be maintained for a long stretch of time. Slow but steady made more sense. He recalled the tale in which Jisdu, the rabbit, trying hard to win a race, ran so fast that eventually, just short of the finish line, he rolled over on his back trying to get his breath. He could go no farther. He could not even stand up. All he could say was *"Mi mi mi."* Carrier did not want to be so foolish as was Jisdu that time. He was in a hurry, but he wanted to get there, accomplish his task and get back. And when he did get back, he wanted to be in fit shape for the furious battle with the *Ani-'squani* which was sure to follow.

He wondered about his mother and his uncle back home in Kituwah. They could not know how much danger he had gotten himself into. Of course, they would be worried about him, but their worries would be general, the kind anyone would have for a loved one on a long and difficult journey alone. They had heard of the existence of the *Ani-'squani*, but to them these strange people were but a rumor, were not real. Just as they had not been real to Carrier until he had actually seen them. Even thinking back on them, after having not only seen them, but having fought them, they did not seem real to Carrier.

He was glad that Dancing Rabbit and his mother did not know what was happening down in the land of the Timucuas and the Calusas. They would worry too much. It would be good enough for them to find out from Carrier himself after he was safely home again, after the danger was past.

He hurried along the path toward his goal. He could not see far ahead, for the path wound its way through dense forest. He did notice that the nature of the forest had changed, and the air was harder to breathe. There was more dampness in the air. There was more water on the ground. In some places, there was water on both sides of the path. And he heard the cries of birds that he had never heard before.

All of a sudden, he felt a tremendous blow across the back of his shoulders, and the impact knocked him sprawling on his face in the path. He rolled quickly onto his back, struggling to get up and defend himself, but a man's foot was on his chest, pushing him back down. Carrier lay back and looked around. There were four men there, all armed, all looking angry. Calusas? he wondered. He thought that he was already in the Calusas' territory.

"Do you speak the trade language?" he asked, using that jargon. No one answered him. They stood there giving him menacing looks. Then it occurred to him that he should speak a few words in his own language. They would not recognize it, of course, and that alone should assure them that he was not one of their local enemies. Their enemies would all live relatively nearby, and these men would recognize the languages of those people. They would not be likely to recognize his.

"*Ayuh Ayunwiyaduh,*" he said, and he saw the men exchange curious glances. Then he repeated his original question, again using the jargon.

"Do you speak the trade language?"

The man standing on his chest stepped back and motioned for Carrier to stand.

"I do," he said. "Who are you?"

Carrier got slowly to his feet. He didn't want to make any quick moves that might cause these men to strike him down again.

"I'm called Carrier," he said, "because of my trade. I carry trade goods long distances."

"I see no trade goods," said the man.

"I lost them up in the land of the Timucuas. I'm one of the

Real People, from farther north—a *Chiloki*. I was going to trade with the Timucuas when I came across the white men. That's when I lost my goods."

"What are you doing here in our land?"

"One of your own people sent me with a message."

"Who sent you," said the other, "and what is the message?"

Carrier hesitated a moment before answering.

"I've been sent by He-Fights-with-Alligators," he said, "to speak with his uncle, Creeping Panther."

Two of the men made audible sounds of astonishment, and all of them looked at each other. Then they stepped back on the path away from Carrier and spoke in low voices in a language that Carrier had never heard before. The man who spoke the trade language moved back toward Carrier.

"What land did you say you came from?"

"I came just now from the land of the Timucuas, your neighbors to the north."

"But that is not your home."

"No. My home is farther north. Beyond the Apalachees and the Muskogees. I'm a Chiloki."

"So you came south to trade with the Timucuas? And is that where you saw He-Fights-with-Alligators?"

"Yes, it is."

"We had long believed that He-Fights-with-Alligators was in the land of the dead. We did not expect to hear that he is in the land of the Timucuas. This is a strange thing for us to hear."

"He's alive," said Carrier, "in the land of the Timucuas."

"Tell us more."

"I was told by He-Fights-with-Alligators to talk to no one except Creeping Panther."

There was another moment of silence. The four Calusas

looked at one another and then back at Carrier. Then the one who had been doing the talking stepped forward again.

"We'll take you to Creeping Panther," he said. "We're from his village. I'm called Swamp-goer. These are my friends. We're all Calusa People."

Twelve

DANCING RABBIT was getting along pretty well on his crutch. If he occasionally got a bit too cocky and tried to put too much weight down on his broken leg, he would be reminded of his invalid status by a sharp pain. But other than that, he could walk just about as far and as long as he wanted to, and pretty quickly, too.

Wasulu was a conjurer, but it was known far and wide that he would do nothing to harm anyone. He used his medicine only for good purposes, and his medicine was strong. Wasulu, or the Tobacco Moth, lived on the outskirts of Kituwah with his wife and four sons, and it was to the home of Wasulu that Dancing Rabbit ventured early one morning, hobbling along at a brisk pace on his crutch.

Dancing Rabbit had of late been worried about his nephew Carrier. There had been no particular reason for his worries. If he had told anyone that he was worried (and he had not told), and if the other had asked him why he worried, he would not have had an answer. Yet he worried.

Then he had dreamed the dream, a frightening dream and one that he could not ignore. He thought that he saw his nephew traveling alone in a strange land pursued by monsters in stone coats. The monsters reminded him of the old tales of Dressed-in-Stone and Flint and Spear-finger and the Gambler, but they were not those monsters. The monsters in Dancing Rabbit's dream were painted white, and their faces were covered with hair. Some of them ran along on four legs. They flung fearful sharp weapons ahead of them, and now and then they spat flames.

The dream had frightened Dancing Rabbit, causing him to awaken in a cold sweat, and therefore he was going to see Wasulu. If anyone would know what to make of the strange dream, Wasulu would. If Carrier was in any real danger, and if anyone could do anything about it, Wasulu would be the one.

Wasulu had an arbor off to the left side of his house, and when Dancing Rabbit came in view of the place, it was under the arbor that he found Wasulu sitting, as if he had been there just waiting for Dancing Rabbit's arrival.

" *'Siyo,* " said Dancing Rabbit.

" *'Siyo,* " said Wasulu. "Come in and sit down. You've had a long walk for a man on only one leg. Or is it that you walk on three?"

Dancing Rabbit hopped his way into the arbor and sat down heavily on a bench opposite where Wasulu sat.

"I walk on two," he said. "The third one hangs there useless."

"I could say the same," said Wasulu. "I think then that you have two just hanging there."

Dancing Rabbit, in spite of his preoccupation with his worries, joined Wasulu in laughter at the joke. After all, one did not just begin talking business at first meeting. Such a thing would be almost as rude as staring at another, and Dancing

Rabbit was always careful to observe the proper etiquette. He was, if possible, even more careful in the presence of a man like Wasulu.

Wasulu, perhaps fifty years old, was young for a man of his profession, especially considering the universally high esteem in which he was held. He had been skinny all his life, but Dancing Rabbit noticed that the conjurer was beginning to develop a little potbelly. Wasulu sat, nearly naked, under the arbor smoking a short clay pipe. A small fire burned on the ground in the center of the arbor.

Dancing Rabbit took his own pipe out of a pouch and filled it with his own tobacco. Wasulu leaned over the fire, picked up a small glowing coal between the tip of his forefinger and his thumb and dropped it into the bowl of Dancing Rabbit's pipe. Dancing Rabbit sucked on the pipe stem to ignite the tobacco, trying not to reveal the amazement he felt at the conjurer's dramatic show.

"*Wado*," he said, and clouds of blue-gray smoke rose up to surround his face. They danced in the slight breeze as they rose to filter themselves through the grass-covered roof of the arbor, then further dissipate on their way to the heavens. The two men smoked in silence for a few more moments, until the pipes went out. Dancing Rabbit put away his own pipe, then he cleared his throat.

"You know my nephew Carrier," he said. It was not a question, but Wasulu answered it just the same.

"Yes," he said. "A fine young man. He used to be called Gnat."

"Yes," said Dancing Rabbit. "That's the one. You know that he's gone south to trade. He's gone alone this time because of my leg, my broken leg. It's the first time he's ever gone out alone, and it's a long trip. He's gone to the land of the Timucuas."

Wasulu nodded his head. "A long way," he said, "through the lands of many different peoples."

"There have been rumors of strange men from across the big waters," said Dancing Rabbit, "men with white skins and hairy faces. South of us. Where my nephew is traveling. I don't know if the rumors are true or not. I don't know even if these strangers are real or not."

"They're real," said Wasulu, "and they're worse than anything you've heard about them. They're worse than you can imagine them to be."

Dancing Rabbit suppressed a shudder that he felt coming from deep inside. He didn't bother to ask Wasulu how he knew that the strangers were real or how he knew so much about them, for he knew that the conjurer had his ways of knowing. After all, that was why he had come to see the man. Instead he went on with his tale.

"Last night," he said, his face grown grim, "I had bad dreams. I saw my nephew running, and behind him came monsters with stone coats and white skins and hairy faces, and some of them ran on four legs. They threw sharp weapons at him, weapons like none that I had ever seen before, and sometimes fire came out of their mouths. That dream bothered me.

"Something has been bothering me for a few days now, but I didn't know what it was until I had that dream. Now I'm worried that what I saw was the strangers that we've heard about, and they're trying to kill my nephew. I'm worried for his safety. That's why I came to see you."

Wasulu refilled and relit his pipe, and he sat and smoked in silence until the pipe was out. He appeared to Dancing Rabbit to be in deep thought, when Dancing Rabbit could see his features through the clouds of smoke. Then Wasulu put the pipe down on his bench and stood up. Over in one corner of the arbor, leaning against the post there was a bow with seven arrows. Wasulu picked them up.

"Wait for me here," he said, and he walked out from under the arbor and started down the path that led from his house to the woods. In a few moments, he had disappeared from the sight of Dancing Rabbit.

The path that Wasulu had taken led him into the woods, and he stayed on the path until he was well into the woods and out of sight of anyone else who might have been watching. Then he stopped. He looked back over his shoulder. He waited for a moment and listened. The only sounds that came to his ears were the chatterings of a squirrel, the songs of various birds and the loud drilling of a large woodpecker somewhere off in the distance. He turned quickly, leaving the path, and began working his way through the thick trees and underbrush.

The going was much slower off the path. Wasulu had to pick his way carefully, for the brush and deadfall underfoot were thick, and the ground was rocky and uneven. And soon he was moving up the side of a hill. The hillside became steeper, and Wasulu's traveling became slower yet, but eventually he reached his goal. It was a small cave in the hillside, almost hidden by large boulders which framed its entrance.

Wasulu sat down with his back against one of the rocks as if to rest, and there he watched, and he waited patiently. Then a rabbit jumped out from behind a tree and sat looking about nervously, twitching its nose. Slowly, Wasulu nocked an arrow and took aim. He let the arrow fly, and it was a good shot. The rabbit flipped over and died almost instantly. It hardly even kicked or twitched. Pleased, Wasulu hurried to its side.

"*Wado*, Jisdu," he said. "I'm sorry to have to kill you, but I have need of your blood."

He stood up and carried the rabbit to the crevasse in the

rocks and laid it there on the ground just to the left of the entrance.

Wasulu had to turn sideways and squeeze himself in between the boulders to get inside the cave. It was dark in there, but he knew what he was after and where to find it, for he himself had put it there. He reached out and felt along the wall of the cave just inside until he touched it, the smooth, cold rim of the large earthen pot. He closed his fingers over its lip and pulled it close to his chest. Clutching it, he slipped back between the rocks to stand outside in the open air again. Then he put the pot on the ground beside the freshly killed rabbit, and he knelt down before it.

Inside the pot was a rolled-up deerskin, and Wasulu pulled it out and slowly rolled it out there on the ground before him to reveal a crystal not much larger than his thumb. Then he turned his attention back to the rabbit. He pulled the arrow on through the warm, soft body, and then, using the sharp flint arrow tip, he slit the throat.

Holding the body of the rabbit up over the crystal, he allowed the fresh, warm, sticky blood to run freely over the stone. *Ulunsuti*, the rare, powerful and dangerous crystal from the forehead of an *uk'ten'*, was being fed. As the final drops drained out of the small body, Wasulu spoke softly, nearly inaudibly, to the object of his attention. Then he put aside the carcass and leaned forward, one hand on each side of *ulunsuti*, and gazed hard and unblinking into the blood-drenched crystal.

He would be a while yet, for he had to watch with patience to see what he could see deep inside of *ulunsuti*, and when at last he had seen, he would have to then rewrap the crystal and find a new hiding place for it to wait in until he had need to call on it again.

He stared hard, and then he began to see the shapes inside

the crystal begin to move, slowly at first, almost impercepti-
bly, then more quickly and more clearly, and then they began
to take on forms both recognizable and meaningful. And there
was nothing more for him to do but watch.

Dancing Rabbit had smoked four pipes, and he had waited for
what had seemed to him like long periods of time between the
smokings. Now and then he had gotten up on his crutch and
haltingly walked around the arbor to get some exercise and to
relieve the boredom. He kept looking toward the path which
Wasulu had taken into the woods, hoping for the conjurer's
return. He knew that these things could not be hurried, yet he
was anxious for the conclusion of this visit.

Then Wasulu's wife had come out of the house and had
brought Dancing Rabbit a bowl of *kanahena* to drink from,
and they had visited awhile. A little later, two of Wasulu's sons
came walking back from somewhere, and they sat and talked
with Dancing Rabbit for a time. Dancing Rabbit was happy to
have the company, for it helped to pass the time, but his mind
was not on the conversations. His mind was on the dreams and
on the fate of Carrier, and he was wishing for the return of the
man who would have the answers to his questions.

Then at last, Wasulu appeared at the edge of the woods.
Breathing hard, carrying by its long ears the body of a rabbit,
he walked slowly and laboriously back toward the arbor. He
handed the rabbit to his wife, and his sons and his wife all went
back inside the house. They knew that he would need privacy
for his consultation with Dancing Rabbit.

Wasulu walked back under the roof of his arbor and sat
down with a long sigh. He put the bow and the arrows down
on the bench beside him. Dancing Rabbit waited patiently for
the conjurer to speak. Instead, Wasulu picked up his pipe and
refilled it. Then he reached down to the fire, as before, for a

coal with which to light his tobacco. He glanced at Dancing Rabbit.

"You have your own tobacco?" he asked.

"Yes."

"Smoke with me."

Dancing Rabbit filled his own pipe with tobacco from his pouch, and again the conjurer plucked a coal from the fire and dropped it in the bowl. The two men then sat across the fire from one another, not looking at one another, there under the arbor, puffing at their pipes, When the pipes at last were done, they knocked the ashes from their bowls into the fire there on the ground. Then at long last Wasulu spoke. His arms were crossed over his bare chest, resting on his belly, and he leaned back slightly and stared over the head of Dancing Rabbit, staring into the far underside of the arbor's roof.

"I looked into *ulunsuti*," he said, "and I saw your nephew there. I saw him old. His hair was white, and his grandchildren played around his feet."

There was nothing more that needed to be said.

Thirteen

THE FOUR CALUSA MEN took Carrier to Creeping Panther and reported to him in their own language. Then Creeping Panther spoke in Swamp-goer's ear in a low voice, and Swamp-goer nodded, turned and walked away. Creeping Panther next spoke briefly to a woman who was standing nearby. Carrier guessed that she was his wife. She turned and walked over to a small fire which was burning in front of a house that stood just behind them and busied herself stirring something in a pot there. Creeping Panther made a gesture indicating that Carrier should follow him.

They climbed up onto the raised floor of the house. The floor was about as high off the ground as was Carrier's waist, and the house had no walls. It was covered over with a roof of thick grass.

Inside the house, if it could be called inside, Creeping Panther motioned toward a bench. Carrier moved to it and sat down. He wondered how he was going to talk to this man. Would Creeping Panther call in an interpreter when he was ready to listen to Carrier's tale? He had sent Swamp-goer away. Swamp-goer at least had been able to talk to Carrier in the trade language. Well, all he could do was sit and wait.

Careful not to stare rudely, Carrier yet managed to get a few glimpses of his host. Creeping Panther was a man of at least middle age. Carrier guessed him to be perhaps as much as sixty years of age, but the man appeared to be strong and healthy. He was tall and lithe. His nearly naked body was completely covered with tattoos, an indication, Carrier thought, of a long and distinguished military career. And the man, in spite of his apparent age, looked as if he could be a formidable opponent yet.

Soon the woman came up into the house, and she gave Carrier a bowl of stew. She offered one to Creeping Panther, but he politely but definitely refused it with a sweep of his hand.

Carrier couldn't identify everything he found in the stew. It was seafood. That much he could tell, and it was very good. He ate his fill, and he thanked the woman, using the trade language. She smiled and nodded, and he couldn't tell whether or not she had actually understood what he had said.

He sat on the bench waiting, and then Creeping Panther spoke. He spoke in the trade language, and Carrier was surprised to find out that he knew it, and having learned that fact, was surprised that the man had not spoken to him earlier.

"They tell me that you have seen my nephew in the country of the Timucuas," said Creeping Panther. "Is that true?"

"In the land of the Timucuas," said Carrier, choosing his words carefully, "I met a man who said that his name is He-Fights-with-Alligators. He said that he is a Calusa, and it was he who sent me here and told me to speak only to you. He said that you are his uncle."

"What was the occasion of your meeting with this man?"

"I am a trader," said Carrier. "I was going to a village of the Timucuas which I had been to before. When I arrived there, I found it occupied by the white men. They chased me. I ran into the forest. Later the man who called himself He-Fights-with-Alligators came upon me in the forest. He said that he had just escaped from those same white men."

Creeping Panther stroked his chin and murmured as if in deep thought. Then he reached for a pouch on the end of his bench.

"Let's smoke," he said, and he took out a pipe and filled it. The woman appeared by his side almost instantly with a glowing faggot from the fire outside, and she held it as Creeping Panther lit the pipe. Then she went out again. Creeping Panther puffed the pipe a few times, then reached across offering it to Carrier. Carrier took it and puffed, then returned it.

"We thought my nephew had been killed long ago," said Creeping Panther, "but it would seem that he was captured instead. If the man you met is indeed my nephew, then he has been a captive of these hairy faces for a long time. Now he's escaped, and you have seen him. That's good. I have one question for you, though."

There was a long pause, and at last, Carrier, nervous, spoke into the uneasy silence.

"Yes?" he said.

"Why did my nephew send you to see me? Why did he not just come home?"

"After we met in the forest," said Carrier, "we found our way to another village of the Timucua people. It was your nephew, if indeed he is your nephew, who led me there. They took us in and fed us and gave us a place to sleep. We decided to help them fight the white men, either kill them or drive them out of the country. We even had one fight with them, but they are still in that village. Your nephew is spying on them. He speaks their language. He's needed there. That's the reason he couldn't come here himself."

Creeping Panther raised his left eyebrow slightly.

"He speaks their language?"

"Yes."

"My nephew was always good with languages. Hmm. And he sent you here to talk to me to what purpose?"

Carrier thought that the others, Swamp-goer and his friends, had most likely already given Creeping Panther the answer to all of these questions. If so, the wily old man was testing Carrier, but Carrier decided that he really couldn't blame him for that. The times were certainly dangerous.

"The white men have weapons that make them hard for us to fight," he said, "and they have the big animals, the ones that carry them on their backs. There are maybe two hundred of these white soldiers. We need more help to fight them and drive them away. Your nephew sent me to ask you to send men to help us fight the strangers."

Creeping Panther handed the pipe back to Carrier, who took it and puffed. The Calusa tobacco mixture was strange, he thought, but good, and it made him feel just a bit light-headed.

"You'll sleep here tonight," said Creeping Panther, suddenly standing up. "In the morning, I'll give you an answer."

That night, when he lay down, Carrier did not sleep right away. He lay awake under the roof of a house with no walls, and he wondered what Creeping Panther would tell him in the morning. The possibilities that entered Carrier's mind ranged from Creeping Panther's total agreement to the request to his deciding to kill Carrier.

Because of his uncertainty regarding his own fate, the fact that he was trying to sleep while completely exposed in the midst of strangers whose attitude toward him was at the least ambiguous made Carrier even more nervous. He kept watching every shadow that moved and squinting into the darkness to try to locate the source of every little sound. He was anxious for Creeping Panther's answer, but of course, he had not expected an immediate answer. He did not know the Calusas, but if they were anything at all like his own people or other people with whom Carrier was familiar, Creeping Panther would not be able to make such an important decision on his own. He would have to consult with someone, at least with a group of advisors or a council, at most with the whole population of his village. Carrier had expected that, but it did not make the waiting or the uncertainty any easier to deal with.

He thought of Potmaker, a captive of those horrible white men. Frightful images of the *'squanis* raced through his mind, and his imagination drew horrid pictures of the helpless Potmaker lying on the ground, the ugly strangers leering and slobbering as they clanked their way closer and closer to her.

At last, he drifted into a deep sleep, and when the noises of the village beginning to stir in the morning woke him up, thankfully, he was not even conscious of having dreamed.

He looked around. People seemed to be going about their business in a completely normal way. He was not exactly being ignored—some people spoke to him—but no one seemed to seek him out either. He could detect no urgency in anyone's behavior. He wondered if perhaps the discussion was still going on somewhere. He did not see Creeping Panther.

He went to the clear running creek nearby and waded in to bathe himself, as was the custom of the Real People, and then he returned to the house in which he had spent the night. He wanted to be found easily when Creeping Panther came looking for him. He wanted to be ready. He was anxious to start back, to get back into the fight, to rescue Potmaker, if her brother had not yet accomplished that task.

It was about mid-morning when the woman he still thought to be Creeping Panther's wife came and offered him food again. He took it gratefully and ate it, and just as he finished eating, Swamp-goer came walking up. He walked with a swagger, but when he spoke he seemed friendly enough. Carrier decided that the swagger was just something in Swamp-goer's nature.

"Is everything all right with you, trader?" said the Calusa.

"I've been treated well enough," said Carrier, "but, no, all will not be well with me until I'm back with my friends and we've killed or driven off the white men."

And until Potmaker is safe and with me, he added, but only to himself. Swamp-goer shrugged and made an ambiguous noise.

"I've not seen Creeping Panther this morning," said Carrier.

"Oh, he'll be here pretty soon, I think," said Swamp-goer. "The big meeting is over with. He's talking just with a few advisors now."

"Have they reached a decision then?" asked Carrier, trying to conceal the anxiety he felt.

"Yes, they have," said Swamp-goer, "but it's not my place to tell you anything about it. You'll have to wait for Creeping Panther. But now, while we wait, there is one who wants to speak with you."

"Of course," said Carrier. "Who is it?"

Swamp-goer looked over his shoulder and gave a nod. A woman Carrier had not noticed before came walking forward, her head down. She stepped up to stand beside Swamp-goer, and she spoke to him in the Calusa language. Swamp-goer answered the woman, then turned toward Carrier and spoke in the trade language.

"This is Blue Crane. She's the wife of He-Fights-with-Alligators," he said. "She wants to know if it's true that you've seen her husband."

"I met a man who told me his name is He-Fights-with-Alligators," said Carrier. He wondered if this was yet another test. "He said that he's Calusa, and that he's been a captive of the white men. He sent me here to speak with Creeping Panther, and he told me that Creeping Panther is his uncle."

There was another exchange between the two Calusas, then Swamp-goer spoke again.

"She wants to know if he's well," he said.

"He's strong and healthy. We had one fight with the white men, and he fought very well, and came through the fight unhurt."

Swamp-goer spoke to Blue Crane again, and she to him.

"Did he have no message for her?" said Swamp-goer.

"No," said Carrier. "He told me only to speak with Creeping Panther."

He saw the hurt expression come over the woman's face when Swamp-goer spoke to her again, and he saw her quickly recover, hide her pain and hold up her head, and her pride and her resilience touched his heart.

"Swamp-goer, my friend," he said, "tell her this. He-Fights-with-Alligators sent no message for his wife, but I think that he's afraid that she has found herself another man. He's afraid that she and all of you thought him dead. That's the reason, I think, that he sent her no message. He told me that. He spoke of her."

As Swamp-goer translated this last, Carrier watched the woman's expression change again, this time to hope, if not quite joy, yet still the change was slight and subtle. Still she stood with pride. She looked at Carrier then and said something which, of course, he did not understand. Then she turned and hurried away.

"She thanked you," said Swamp-goer.

"She has not remarried?" Carrier asked.

"No. When others said that her man was dead, she said that she did not believe it. She has refused several men who wanted her since he disappeared."

"My friend will be glad to hear that, I think," said Carrier, and for a moment there was silence. Swamp-goer broke it with a suddenness.

"Ah," he said, looking over Carrier's shoulder, "here comes Creeping Panther."

Carrier turned around to face Creeping Panther as he approached. Within a few steps of the two men who waited, Creeping Panther spoke to Swamp-goer, but this time he spoke in the trade tongue so that Carrier could understand.

"Have you told him?" he asked.

"No. We waited for you."

"Carrier," said Creeping Panther, "it's been decided. We will help you. We'll help because of my nephew and because the Timucuas are our neighbors and the white men are all our enemies. The word has gone out, and the men are to gather here. One hundred of us will follow you back to the Timucua village from which you came. We'll leave here as soon as they all arrive."

Fourteen

WHEN THE ROUGH HANDS of the bearded white man had grabbed her from behind, Potmaker had thought for sure that she would soon be dead. But even as the fight had continued raging around them, the man had pulled her close to him and held her tightly against the smooth, hard metal shirt. He had dragged her away from the fight, dragged her backward, kicking, struggling to free her arms. Even as she fought against him, she noticed the rank odor of his body, and she felt the face hair against her bare back. She saw only the huge hands that gripped her tightly around the arms, so tightly that her own hands were already beginning to tingle from the diminished blood flow, and the hands that gripped her were hairy with thick reddish hair.

He had dragged her away from the fight and back to the village, her own village which the strangers had occupied, still occupied, after chasing her and her people away so many days before, and there he had taken her into a house and thrown her down on the ground. She had hurriedly rolled over on her back to face him. He was standing in the doorway. She came quickly to her feet in a fighting stance and reached for the flint knife which was still sheathed at her waist, but before she could draw it out, he had stepped forward and slapped her viciously across the face.

She fell back again on the packed dirt floor, and he came down hard on top of her, knocking the wind out of her lungs. He straddled her upper body, his legs below the knees holding down her arms. She struggled still, frantically, but his weight and his strength were soon too much for her. He slapped her brutally across the face again, and then he reached back to take her knife out of its sheath and toss it away. It was her last weapon.

Finally, nearly exhausted, she had all but stopped struggling, and then he had stood up and backed slowly a little ways away from her. Still he blocked her way to the door.

Then he reached up with both hands and removed the hideous helmet from his head and tossed it aside, and only then did she see what he really looked like. He grinned at her, and his yellow teeth showed through the thick red hair which covered most of his face. His eyes were mostly red, as if, she thought, someone had poked a finger into them. The hair on his head was curly and matted.

He continued taking off pieces of his armor or clothing and tossing them aside, and then she realized what it was that he intended to do with her and why he had not killed her in the first place. She stood up and ran for the door, and he grabbed her again and threw her to the ground.

At first she had fought, but as the days went by and the filthy, hairy men had taken their turns, after she had suffered several beatings trying to resist their disgusting advances, she had at last given in, and after that when one of them came for her, she complacently complied.

She hated these men worse than ever before, and she had long since resolved to await her chance, not only to escape, but to kill at least one of them in the process. And she fantasized about the killing, imagined it over and over again in graphic and gory detail.

She knew that in order to survive and to accomplish her purpose, she would have to be patient and endure. Of course, she also held on to the hope that her own people would rescue her, either by sneaking in quietly some night to free her or by an open attack on the village.

And she imagined that the trader from the north, the one called Carrier, would be one of the strongest voices in favor of such an attempt, that he would even be the leader of the rescue mission. She had seen him watching her, and she knew how he felt about her. But then, she wondered if he would feel the same way after he had learned of the way in which the white men had been using her.

And even if Carrier did not lead such an effort, then Tree Frog, her brother, would surely do so. She was ashamed of herself that she had allowed the red-haired man to catch her from behind and carry her off so easily, to put her in this position where she must wait for men to make up their minds about what to do and to figure out the best way to do it. Perhaps, after all, she would have to wait for the right moment and escape on her own.

Since she had stopped fighting the white men, they had relaxed their watch on her somewhat. They had given her certain chores to do around the village, and while she was doing those things, they more or less ignored her. Of course, if she wandered too near the edge of the village, someone would yell at her in their harsh, strange language or threaten her with a gesture, but other than that, she was moving about rather freely. And she gave them no outward sign of her desperate interest in escape. She went about her business with a slow, seemingly lethargic attitude.

One day, she kept telling herself, she would see her opportunity, and when that day came, she would take full advantage of it. As she carried wood, built fires, cooked food or washed clothes, she would see a chance to pick up and secret away a weapon of some kind, a knife, a club, a sharp stick, anything, and then she would wait patiently a while longer until the opportunity to make use of the weapon came her way. And it would come. Sooner or later, one way or another, it would come. So if Carrier and Tree Frog and all the others should fail to come to her rescue, she would take care of the problem for herself.

He-Fights-with-Alligators watched the camp of the Españols day after day. He got as close to the occupied village as he dared to get, for in addition to watching the Españols, he hoped to be able to listen to them. Most of the time he was unable to do that. Now and then he could understand some shouted word or phrase, but usually he was too far away to understand anything the men were saying, and when he did manage to hear, it was something of no consequence.

He did see where they were keeping the young woman, the sister of Tree Frog, and after his first day of watching and listening, he had gone back to the others to report on the things that he had seen.

"Your sister is still alive," he had told Tree Frog. "She's their captive in the village."

"Is she well?" asked Tree Frog.

"As far as I can tell, she's well and unhurt, but the Españols do not treat their captives well. They treat them as slaves, and they are cruel masters."

The bitterness that He-Fights-with-Alligators carried with

him from his own years of captivity showed in his face and could be heard in his voice.

"We have to get her away from them," said Tree Frog.

"Yes, and soon," said He-Fights-with-Alligators. "If we can."

He ate, and then he went back to his post. After several days, he could report nothing of any significance going on in the occupied village. The white men had cleaned all their weapons. There had been some movement of men back and forth between the village and the big boats which were still resting in the waters back along the coast. But there had been no indication of any plans to leave the village, either for the boats or for further inland excursions.

"I can tell nothing," he reported back to the Timucuas, "except that they appear to be planning to stay."

Tree Frog made an announcement.

"We will attack the village," he said.

The Timucuas, He-Fights-with-Alligators among them, attacked the village from all sides at once. They surprised the unsuspecting strangers. There were guards posted, but it seemed that they were routinely posted and were not particularly expecting any real trouble. They were certainly not expecting the kind of attack which they received.

Shark Tooth led one group down the road from the east. Tree Frog and another group had circled the village to approach from the west. Two other groups had gone into the forest on either side of the road in order to attack, one from the north and the other from the south. At a signal from Tree Frog, a long call like the sound of a whooping crane, they all charged at once, screaming, shrieking, shouting.

The guards were the first to fall, and the enemy camp was thrown into immediate disarray. White men ran for their weapons. Some ran for their big animals. Arrows fell like rain into the village, and some white men fell, screaming in agony, punctured at random by several shafts. A few of the big animals screamed hideously, also stabbed by arrows.

It looked at first as if it would be a complete rout by the Timucua forces, but many of the white men had gotten themselves into the houses and, therefore, to their weapons. The Timucuas were in the village, and there was hand-to-hand fighting. Tree Frog crushed the skull of a big hairy-faced man with a powerful blow of his heavy ball-headed warclub.

As Shark Tooth was rushing past a house, a half-naked white man stepped out the door, sword in hand, and with one mighty swipe of his blade, nearly took the head off Shark Tooth's shoulders. The Timucua ran a few more steps before he fell, and He-Fights-with-Alligators shot an arrow into the hairy belly of the man who had killed him.

Inside another house, Potmaker was braced for an assault of another kind when the first sounds of attack split the air. She and the man were both naked when they heard the shouts. The man turned and ran to the door to look out. As he did, Potmaker ran to the weapons belt he had laid aside. She pulled his sharp knife from its sheath and stepped up behind him.

He saw what was happening, turned back to go for his clothes and his weapons, and just as he turned, she was there. Before he had a chance to shout at her or to slap her aside, he felt the blade slide so smoothly, so easily, up through the overhang of his belly, up into his guts. It was cold inside him, and it was hard and smooth. He gasped. He started to growl, and his hands moved upward, intending to grasp her by the throat, but before they could reach her, she sliced upward, opening him up clear to his sternum. As his innards spilled and a horrid stench exuded from the cavernous wound, Potmaker, still clutching the knife, stepped back and to one side. The body pitched forward. She stepped over it and into the doorway.

Looking out, she saw the battle raging, and she ran screaming to join it. Before the day was done, she had killed two more, but then the Timucuas began losing heavily to the loud blowguns of the enemy, firing from inside the houses. Grabbing up the bodies of their own fallen warriors, they beat a hasty retreat.

The next several days were taken up by mourning for the dead and purification rites for those who had helped to do the killing. There were also wounds to be tended, and, of course, the road had to be watched for any sign of counterattack. He-Fights-with-Alligators, after a brief respite, went back to his hiding place near the village to continue spying.

"The Españols," he had said, "will never let an attack go unpunished. They will come for us. Probably soon."

After going through her own purification, and after having bathed several times in the river, Potmaker found her brother.

"Where is that trader from the north?" she asked him.

"You mean Carrier, the Chiloki?" he responded.

"Yes. That one."

"He's gone to the Calusas. He-Fights-with-Alligators sent him to talk to his uncle and bring some Calusas up here to help us in this fight. Carrier wanted to stay and fight. He wanted to find you. But we told him that He-Fights-with-Alligators is the only one who knows these white men, so he couldn't go. And one of us couldn't go, because the Calusas might not trust us. He had to go."

"Oh," said Potmaker, "I see."

And she was glad to discover that Carrier had not had a choice, that he had been more or less forced to abandon her and to leave her fate in the hands of her brother. But now she worried for his safety. What dangers would there be on his journey? And how would he be received by the unpredictable Calusas?

He-Fights-with-Alligators watched the Españols. They were angry. They were preparing for battle. It would not be long before they would be ready to attack. He knew these men, knew them well, and he knew that when the reprisal came it would be brutal beyond imagination. He and the Timucuas had hurt them, and worse, they had humiliated them. The Españols would not stand for that.

And he knew that it was too much to hope that Carrier would get back with reinforcements from Creeping Panther in time. No. They would have to prepare to meet this attack as they were. Or they would have to find a way to avoid it.

Fifteen

CARRIER WALKED alongside Creeping Panther at the head of the long column of Calusas who followed on the trail back toward the land of the Timucuas to the north, the trail which would lead them to the field of battle where they would kill or be killed by the monstrous invaders from across the waters, the men with colorless skin and hairy faces and bodies, the men with metal armor and weapons who rode on the backs of huge four-legged beasts and who crossed the waters in giant boats.

They moved along at a quick pace, but it could not have been fast enough for Carrier. Carrier wanted to be back with the Timucuas. He worried about the safety of Potmaker. But his longings went beyond her immediate safety and included his future and hers, their future together. It was not, he thought, too much to hope for, not too much if he could only get back in time.

He longed to be back among the Timucuas to fight and kill the hateful invaders. He had gotten a taste of battle with the

Ani-Asquani, as he called them, trying his best to render in his own language the name he had heard applied to them by He-Fights-with-Alligators. He had gotten a taste of battle with them, and he longed for more. He needed more. He craved victory over these seemingly inhuman forces.

He was anxious to be far enough north to be out of this place where he seemed to be always surrounded by water and by the strange creatures which inhabited it: birds, snakes, lizards, even small four-footed hairy animals he had never seen before and had no word with which to name them. Of course there were some he knew, but there were many more he did not.

But most of all, he found himself longing for all of this to be over and done with: the return trip to the Timucua land, the fight with the *Ani-'squani*, his own return trip back to his home. He wanted to be back home, and he wanted to be there with Potmaker as his new wife. He imagined, as he traveled the trail through the swamplands beside Creeping Panther, a scene at Kituwah when he arrived back home. His uncle, Dancing Rabbit, pleased and astonished to see him, he introducing to his mother and to Dancing Rabbit his new wife, the bold and beautiful Potmaker of the Timucuas.

No. The pace could not be too fast for Carrier. He was impatient with Creeping Panther. He himself felt as if he could run without a pause for rest all the way back and then jump right into a fight.

When He-Fights-with-Alligators saw the Españols putting the saddles on their animals, he knew that the time had come. He eased himself down out of the tree in which he had been perched and backed quietly through the forest until he felt that he was a safe distance away. Then he turned and ran.

He ran the trail that he had learned so well by this time, the trail that led through the forest and back to the village of Big Mouth. He ran as fast as he could, for he ran with a sense of urgency, and he made the trip in better time than he had made it before. He charged into the village, which was still in some disarray, for the mourning was not yet completely accomplished, nor was the purification. Wounded were still in pain, some disabled, and Big Mouth had not yet been officially replaced as town chief. No one was in charge. No one was in control.

Yet the situation called for immediate response. There would be no time for formal or official organization. He-Fights-with-Alligators ran to the center of the village there before the large townhouse, and he cried out to all who could hear.

"Listen to me. Listen to me. The white men are coming. The white men are coming here to attack."

It didn't take long for a crowd to gather around the Calusa, and Potmaker and her brother Tree Frog were right there in front.

"How soon will they be here?" someone asked.

"They were getting ready when I left. They'll be here soon."

"Get your weapons," someone shouted.

"Should we meet them here or on the road?" said another.

Tree Frog stepped up to stand beside He-Fights-with-Alligators, and he held up his hands for silence. It took a moment, but finally the crowd complied. Then Tree Frog looked at the Calusa standing there by his side, a onetime enemy, now his most trusted ally.

"What do you think we should do?" he asked.

"We're not ready to fight them again. Not yet. And not here. You'll have to abandon this village and hide in the forests or go to other villages."

"I think that our Calusa friend is right," Tree Frog said to the crowd. "Take your weapons and help the wounded. Let's all leave this village at once. Scatter through the forest. Let's all meet in four days at the village of Big Conch."

People ran to their houses to gather what belongings they could, weapons, other things they thought they would need. Mothers yelled for their children. Dogs yapped and ran in confusion at the strange activity around them. People with wounded relatives helped them along, and in a very short time, small groups of three to seven people each were running or hobbling into the forest in different directions from different locations in the village. Potmaker, Tree Frog and He-Fights-with-Alligators were soon the only ones left. They looked around to make sure that everyone else was gone.

"You come with us," said Tree Frog.

"No. You two go on. I'll stay and watch to see what the Españols will do."

"Then we'll all stay," said Potmaker.

"It's easier for one to hide," the Calusa protested.

"The forest is thick around the edge of this village," said Potmaker. "It can hide many."

He-Fights-with-Alligators started to protest further, but Tree Frog interrupted him.

"It takes more time to argue than to hide," he said.

The Calusa heaved a sigh, nodded once and said, "All right."

Then the three of them began to look around.

"What will the white men do, do you think," said Potmaker, "when they arrive and find the village abandoned?"

"They might search a little ways into the forest," said He-Fights-with-Alligators, "but if they go very far, I think they'll go by the road. Their caballos, that's what they call their beasts, are too large to be useful in the forest."

"Then we should go into the forest to hide," said Tree Frog.

"Yes," said He-Fights-with-Alligators, and he leaned back his head to look up into the lofty branches above, "but up there, I think."

"Come on then," said Tree Frog, and the three of them ran out of the village to the base of a large tree at the edge of the forest. The leaves on its branches were lush and thick and would hide them easily, and the tall old tree stood in an ideal location to overlook the approach to the village from the west.

Tree Frog went up first, then Potmaker followed. He-Fights-with-Alligators was the last to climb, and as he started inching his way up the trunk toward the lowest branch, he could hear the distant clatter of the approaching Españols. He was well into the branches, though, before the white men arrived at the village.

Then the mounted men clattered into the abandoned village, and the sight and the sound of them were frightful to Potmaker even from her well-hidden perch high above. There was no life in the village except for a few stray dogs who had failed to follow the people when they left.

The invaders, apparently frustrated at finding yet another abandoned village, ran the dogs through with their long lances. They rode angrily up and down the village streets, stabbing and slashing at empty houses, shouting in their unintelligible language, unintelligible to Potmaker and her brother, but not, she recalled, to the Calusa who was their companion.

Then the one who seemed to be their leader shouted something, and one of the men rode over to a spot where a small fire still burned in front of one of the houses. He poked the tip of his long lance into the fire and flicked it toward the house.

Soon the house was burning. Other men imitated his action or grabbed flaming faggots from the burning house and hurled them at other houses.

In a short while the entire village was ablaze. The leader shouted again, and six of the mounted men rode out of the village on the road that continued inland. If they rode far enough, they would come to another village, Potmaker knew. The road would eventually lead them to the village of Big Conch. She hoped that they would not ride that far. Some of the refugees from this village would almost certainly have gone there for safety.

Then other men rode the large beasts all around the edge of the clearing in which the village was located. Peering into the trees and poking their lances into the thick underbrush, at one point they prowled just under where the three fugitives perched overhead.

It seemed to Potmaker that these men would stay around forever, but at last, at another shout from their leader, they turned their beasts and headed back down the road toward the village which they occupied, Potmaker's own village. The six who had gone east on the inland road returned then and took up the rear on their disappointed return trip.

Potmaker and the two men with her in the tree waited until they could no longer hear the sounds of the animals' hoofs or the clatter of the metal or the raspy voices of the invaders. Then He-Fights-with-Alligators spoke in a harsh whisper.

"It's safe now, I think," he said. "Let's go on down. One at a time. I'll go first."

On the ground again they surveyed for a silent moment the ruins of the still smoldering village. They looked down the road in the direction the enemy had gone. All was silent. All was still. The smell of the burning houses filled their nostrils, and smoke rose from the heaps of ashes that only a short while before had been homes to families.

"What do we do now?" asked Potmaker, breaking the uneasy silence.

"I'll go back to what I was doing before," said He-Fights-with-Alligators. "I'll watch the Españols and try to hear what they say. I don't think they'll go away. I think the next time they'll plan for a longer trip. They'll pack some food, and they won't turn around and go back so soon. They'll keep riding through the forest on this road until they find someone to kill or capture. I should keep watching them."

"All right," said Tree Frog, "but what will happen now when Carrier returns, hopefully with your people? He'll be coming back here to look for us, and he'll find this village abandoned and destroyed."

"One of us should stay here and wait for him," said Potmaker.

"You're right, of course," said the Calusa.

"I'll stay here," said Tree Frog. "Sister, you go on to the village of Big Conch. When the time comes, we'll find you there." He turned toward He-Fights-with-Alligators. "Do you know how to get to that village?"

"Yes. It's just down the road here."

"Good. Then it's all decided. You two go on. I'll see you both later in the village of Big Conch."

"Wait," said Potmaker, putting a hand on her brother's arm. "You go to Big Conch's village. I'll stay here and wait for Carrier."

Tree Frog started to say something in protest, but looking at his sister's face, he hesitated. He turned toward He-Fights-with-Alligators, but the Calusa only shrugged.

"It takes more time to argue," he said, "than to just go

ahead and do it. I'm going. One of you should stay here and wait for Carrier."

He turned and trotted off to disappear into the forest. Tree Frog turned back toward his sister.

"I don't want to go to the village," she said. "I don't want to be around the others just yet. I want to be by myself. You go on and tell them what we're doing."

"Be careful," said Tree Frog. "Stay well hidden. What will you find to eat?"

"The white men didn't find all the food storage places," she said. "There's still food here. I'll be all right."

"Then I'll go," said Tree Frog. "When Carrier comes, bring him to the village of Big Conch. I'll be there waiting for you."

In another moment, she was there alone, the ruins of a village there before her. She thought of her own village, a ruin of another kind, occupied by the hateful strangers. She would not live there again. She would rather see it also in ashes. Nothing but fire, she thought, would rid it of the horrible stench of what had gone on there.

Then she thought of the village of Big Conch. That would be the next one the white men would encounter. If they decided to venture farther, they would be there next. She hoped that it would not wind up like either of the first two. She hoped that Carrier would get back with reinforcements from the Calusas before the white men decided to go out again.

And if the reinforcements did arrive in time, she wondered, would they, even then, be able to defeat these men with their strange animals and strange weapons? Or would this be the end, the end of life as she knew it? She wondered, and she was afraid, and she realized then all of a sudden that she was longing for the company of Carrier. She longed to ask him for answers to the questions that were troubling her. She longed to know what he thought about the strange and troubling things that were happening to them.

She heaved a heavy sigh and turned to walk back into the forest to look for a suitable place to settle in to wait and watch.

Sixteen

TAKING THE LEAD, Carrier left the main road and led Creeping Panther and the other Calusas off on a narrow trail which he knew would take him back to the village of Big Mouth. It was the way He-Fights-with-Alligators had shown him so that he could avoid any chance of meeting up with the *Ani-'squani* along the way. It was not far from that point back to the village of Big Mouth. He glanced back over his shoulder to speak to Creeping Panther.

"It's not far now," he said.

They moved in single file because the trail had become so narrow. Even so, with Carrier leading the way, they moved faster than they had before. Carrier hurried ahead, and no one said anything to him to try to slow him down. They just picked up their own pace in order to keep up with him.

Potmaker heard the sound of a large number of people approaching. They were coming from the south along the narrow trail, and they were not clanking or making the other loud noises that the strangers seemed always to make. She thought that it must be Carrier returning with the Calusas, but she couldn't be sure, so she hid herself and waited. Safely concealed, she watched, and then she saw them. It was indeed Carrier, and he was leading many men, Calusas, she was sure.

Carrier raced into the clearing where the village had been, but all he could see was ashes. He looked around quickly in desperation.

"We're too late," he cried. "They've been here before us. The hairy-faced white men have been here and burned everything."

"There are no bodies here," said Creeping Panther. "It would seem that the people all escaped. Is this the place you've brought us to?"

Carrier started to try to explain, but just then Potmaker came out of her hiding place and ran toward him.

"You're safe," Carrier said.

"Yes. My brother and others attacked the white men, and I was able to escape during the fight."

"But what are you doing here? What has happened here?"

"The white men came to get even with us. Everyone ran away, so there was no fight here, but they burned the village when they found it abandoned. They made sure that no one had any homes to come back to."

"And you're here alone?"

"Yes. We knew that you'd be coming here. Someone had to meet you. So I stayed."

"Where are the others?"

"They've gone to various villages. Some might be hiding in the forest. We're to meet in the village of Big Conch."

"I don't know where that is," said Carrier.

"I can take you there."

Then there was an awkward pause, and Carrier became

suddenly aware of his failure to observe the proper etiquette. He had been shocked at the sight of the ashes, then excited at the appearance of Potmaker, and he had been full of questions. He had not made introductions. He turned toward Creeping Panther.

"Creeping Panther," he said, "this is Potmaker of the Timucuas. She fought with us against the white men, and she was captured. She's a brave fighter.

"Potmaker, this is Creeping Panther of the Calusas. He's come back with me and brought all these men to help us in our fight."

"You're the uncle of He-Fights-with-Alligators?" said Potmaker.

"Yes. I am."

"You're welcome here. I wish I was better prepared to show you Timucua hospitality, but I'm sure that will be taken care of at Big Conch's village."

"Shall we go then?" said Creeping Panther. "I'm anxious to see my nephew."

"Your nephew's not at the village. He's watching the white men. He understands their language."

"Can we go get him?" asked Carrier.

"I think that would be dangerous," said Potmaker. "I think we should go to Big Conch's village and wait for him there. When he learns something, he'll go there to meet us. He knows where it is."

Carrier gave Creeping Panther a questioning look.

"Let's go to the village of Big Conch," said Creeping Panther.

From where He-Fights-with-Alligators hid and watched, he saw the captains all go to the house where Francisco de Garay himself had settled in. He knew that Garay must be about to conduct a major conference with his officers, and he wanted to hear what they would have to say. The house in which Garay was staying was close to the edge of the village, and if he was careful, the Calusa thought, he could inch up close to the back of the house. Maybe he would be able to hear the voices through the back wall.

Slowly he moved toward the house, and then he saw the sentry posted outside the back wall. He dropped down to all fours and crept closer, moving slowly and as quietly as possible. The sentry turned and paced a couple of steps away. His back was turned to He-Fights-with-Alligators. The Calusa inched forward some more, then stood up, drawing the knife out of its sheath at his waist. He would have to do this quietly.

When he made his move, it was sudden. He stepped quickly up behind the sentry, reaching around the man's head with his left hand and clamping it over the mouth. At the same time, he shoved the flint blade into the man's throat and ripped it to the side.

There was a gurgle and a sigh but nothing more, nothing more until the dying hand released its grip on the long lance it held. The lance clattered to the ground. He-Fights-with-Alligators eased the body down to the ground beside it and held his breath, waiting. A voice came from inside the house, speaking through the back wall.

"¿Tiburcio? ¿Tiburcio?"

He-Fights-with-Alligators took a deep breath.

"A sus órdenes, mi coronel!" he said.

"¿Hay una problema?"

"Todo anda tranquilo."

He breathed a little more easily when the conversation ended there. Apparently no one was suspicious. He was glad for the first time that he had spent enough time with the Españols to learn their language well. He stood close to the wall and listened, and he heard the voice of Francisco de Garay.

"Estos salvajes merecen una lección."

"Sí, mi capitán," answered one of the captains.

"¿Pensáis que podremos marcharnos dentro de siete días?"

"Sí, Capitán."

"La mitad de la compañía se quedará aquí. Teniente Lucas, haga los arreglos."

"¡De immediato, mi capitán!"

He-Fights-with-Alligators decided that he had heard enough and that he would be pushing his luck too much to stay around any longer. He moved quietly and cautiously back into the forest and continued in that manner until he was well back from the village. Then he turned to hurry the rest of the way to the village of Big Conch.

The Calusas were welcomed at the village of Big Conch, and Big Conch himself called for a feast to be prepared. Creeping Panther especially was treated as a special guest, someone of great importance, and it was obvious that he enjoyed his status and all the attention it brought him.

The first chance he got, Carrier made his way to the side of Potmaker.

"I'm glad that you escaped unharmed," he said. "All the time I was gone, I thought about you. I wanted to go to help you, but they told me I had to go talk to Creeping Panther."

"They were right, of course," said Potmaker, "and after all, it all worked out. But I'm glad you thought of me."

"Among my people," said Carrier, "when two people wed, the man goes to live with the woman's people. That's the ordinary way. But I have to go back to my own people."

He was thinking about the writing and the necessity of keeping it for the Real People, even though it had to be kept a secret for some time. The importance of all that had been strongly impressed upon his mind since he was a child by his uncle Dancing Rabbit. He could not abandon the mission he had accepted.

"Even though it's not the ordinary way," he continued, "it would please me very much if you would be willing to go back with me when the time comes."

"You want me to go back with you to your people?"

"Yes. As my wife."

It occurred to Carrier that he was being brash and impulsive. This was not the proper way to do things. But then, the times and the circumstances in which he found himself were far from ordinary. He felt a need to explain himself.

"With these white men here and all the fighting going on," he said, "one of us or both of us could be killed any day. Perhaps that's the reason I feel the need to speak so soon."

Potmaker grew somber. She looked thoughtful, almost troubled.

"I like you, Carrier," she said. "If we live through this fight, let's talk about this some more."

Carrier woke up the following morning to the sound of the voice of Creeping Panther shouting with joy.

"It's my nephew. My nephew is here."

By the time Carrier got up and out into the street a small crowd had already gathered around the two Calusas. Uncle and nephew embraced.

"I didn't know whether to believe it or not until just now," said Creeping Panther. "We had assumed you dead for so long."

"It's good to see you, Uncle. Thank you for coming. You brought men to fight?"

"Yes."

"Good. They'll be needed soon. We can talk later. Right now I have some things to report to Big Conch."

Big Conch stepped forward just then.

"At the townhouse," he said. "We'll hear you there. Everyone can come and listen."

The townhouse was filled, but everyone was quiet. Big Conch sat in his seat of honor, and he invited Creeping Panther to sit beside him. He-Fights-with-Alligators stood to speak.

"I listened to the Españols," he said, "the white men. They are angry. They want to teach us that they're our masters. They are going to take seven days to prepare for a journey. Then they'll be coming this way. If we abandon this village, they'll burn it like they did the other, but they'll keep looking for us this time. They won't go back. They won't be satisfied until they've found us. This time, I think, they'll even ride into the forests looking for us if they have to.

"They're packing food and supplies for a long trip. That's why it will take them seven days to get ready. Half of them will ride toward us to fight and half will stay behind. This is what I heard them say, and I came running straight back here to tell it. That's all I have to say."

He-Fights-with-Alligators sat down, and Big Conch stood up. He looked over the crowd, which included his own people, the refugees from other Timucua villages, the Calusas who had come north with Creeping Panther, and, of course, the trader from the land of the Chilokis even farther to the north. He drew himself up tall and took a deep breath.

"My brothers and sisters," he said, "our visiting friends and allies, I think we do not need to wait for these arrogant strangers to come into our country and attack us. Our Calusa friend here has done well. We know that the enemy will be spending the next seven days in preparation for travel. We have great strength. We have our own strength and the strength of our Calusa friends. Let's surprise them while they're getting ready for their trip. Let's attack them. Let's drive them out or kill them off."

Creeping Panther stood to speak next. He spoke in the trade language which many of the Timucuas understood.

"I agree with Big Conch," he said. "We Calusas came up here ready to fight. My nephew has told us what the enemy is doing. Now is the time to strike."

Several others spoke, but no one spoke in opposition. Each speaker only reiterated what had been said before. The decision was made. As the meeting broke up, Big Conch motioned to Creeping Panther.

"You and I and your nephew," he said, "will meet together and decide a battle plan."

He-Fights-with-Alligators, who had overheard, said, "I think that Tree Frog and Carrier should join us."

"It's good," said Big Conch. "Go get them and bring them here."

M.J.

Seventeen

OF COURSE it was much too soon yet to know for sure, but Potmaker had a feeling. It was the kind of feeling that she could not have explained, not even to another woman, but even so it was a strong and distinct feeling. It was a deep feeling that she was going to have a child. She was going to have a child by one of the hairy-faced white men. She could not know which one. There was no way she could know that. She wondered if her child would have hair on its face.

She also wondered what Carrier would think about her when he found out about the child. She had not even told him what the white men had done with her—to her. She wanted to go back with Carrier, as he had asked her to do, to the land of his people, the people they called in the trade language the Chilokis, but she had not answered him when he had asked her. She had not answered him because of this feeling she had, and because she did not know how he would react to that information.

She had told him to wait until the problem with the strangers was resolved, to wait until the fight was over and done. She had said that they would talk of it again if they both survived the coming big fight.

But if they did, what would she say then? Would she be any more ready to talk to him then than she had been before? Would she tell him about the white men and what they had done to her? Would she tell him about her feeling? And if she did tell him, what would he say then? Would he still want her to go with him?

And what if a child really did come? What then? Would she keep it? She didn't know. She could prevent its birth. Even after the birth, she could still kill the infant if she chose to do so. That was her right. It would be her child. No one else's.

But she did not know what she would do. She wondered what it would look like. She wondered what Carrier would think about it. A child born of hatred and violence. A child of the hated invaders. What would it be like? What would Carrier think? Would he want to kill it? What if she decided to keep it and raise it? What would her own people, including her own brother, think of that?

Carrier wandered alone along the edge of the forest just behind the village. It was late evening, and the plans had already been made for the attack on the *Ani-'squani*. They would be leaving in the early morning. Carrier was ready to go, and he was not yet ready to retire for the night. So he wandered alone.

He knew that his thoughts should be on the coming fight, but they were not. He was thinking of the beautiful Potmaker. He had never yet seen a woman he wanted so badly as he wanted this one. She had been in his thoughts almost since the first time he had seen her. When she was out of his sight, he tried to envision her. He tried to imagine the feel of her skin.

He wondered why she had not given him an answer to his question. Perhaps she did not feel about him the way he felt about her. But she had said that she liked him, and she had said that they should talk about it further. Was it then because he had not followed the proper procedures? It might have been, but he did not think so. Perhaps it was because she thought that one of them might be killed in the coming fight. She had said that they should talk about it again after the fight was over. Then again, maybe she just didn't like the idea of leaving her home. He couldn't blame her for that. He himself couldn't think about staying away from his own people.

But Carrier wasn't really satisfied with any of those possible answers to his question. There must be something else he was not thinking of, some other possible reason for her hesitation. He wondered if he should speak to her brother Tree Frog about his desires—and about his confusion.

Strange, he realized, but he did not know if Potmaker had any family other than her brother. He had not met any other, no parents, no other brothers or sisters, no one. Not an uncle or an aunt. Could there be just the two of them? He decided that he would speak to Tree Frog the first chance he got.

Back in the village, He-Fights-with-Alligators and his uncle Creeping Panther sat side by side in front of one of the houses. A small fire burned on the ground there in front of them. Creeping Panther filled a pipe and lit it with a burning stick from the fire, then carefully replaced the stick. He puffed on the pipe a few times and handed it to his nephew.

"It does my heart good to see you again, alive and well," he said. "It had been such a long time since you were taken away. Everyone had given up, just about. All of us thought that you were dead. All of us, that is, except your wife. She never gave up."

"My wife?"

"She always said that you'd come back to us. Several times men tried to marry her. They said that you must be dead and that she had a right to take another husband, but she always refused them and said that you'd be back."

"That makes me very happy, Uncle," said He-Fights-with-Alligators. He puffed thoughtfully on the pipe, then handed it back to his uncle. "I tried not to think about her, because I was afraid that she would believe me dead and take another man. This—what you have just told me—is almost too much to hope for."

"Nevertheless, it is true. Blue Crane is waiting for you at home."

He-Fights-with-Alligators suddenly stood up and paced nervously away from the fire. When he stopped, he stood facing in the direction of the village occupied by the enemy. He stared off into the darkness in silence for a long pause before he spoke again.

"We cannot kill these Españols fast enough to suit me," he said. "I long to be back home with my wife."

Men, and some women, including Potmaker, prepared their weapons. Some sang and some prayed. The conjurers were busy with rituals designed to make up in some way for the lack of the ordinary long-term preparation for warfare. They appealed to the spirits for understanding. The situation, they explained, was not an ordinary one. They had been invaded by a strange and brutal people from some faraway land. The normal rules of warfare were suspended. They begged the spirits to have mercy on them, to forgive them for their abbreviated rituals.

Big Conch spent the night alone praying his own private prayers for success in the battle which the morning would bring. Even though there would be people from other villages and even a strong force of Calusas involved, the attack was being launched from his village. He was responsible. The success or failure would be all on his shoulders.

It was late when Carrier walked back into the village and searched out Tree Frog. He found him sitting alone just outside the townhouse. He hesitated, though, to approach his friend. Tree Frog might want to be left alone with his thoughts or his prayers. He could be preparing himself in his own private, quiet way for the battle to come. Carrier stood back and waited, and soon Tree Frog looked up and saw him there.

"Hello, my friend," said Tree Frog. "Smoke with me?"

"Yes," said Carrier. "Thank you."

He walked over and sat down beside Tree Frog, who was by then preparing a pipe. They sat and smoked without talking, and when the pipe was done, Tree Frog put it away. Only then did he break the silence.

"I wonder what tomorrow will bring," he said. "I wonder if the two of us will sit and smoke together like this again."

"It's a hard thing to think about," said Carrier. "No matter what the outcome, there will be some who will not survive tomorrow's fight."

"And many of them will be white men," said Tree Frog, his wistful mood abruptly changing to one of determination.

"Yes. And you and I will account for at least our fair share."

There was a long pause, and the silence was almost ominous. The two young men sat side by side staring at the ground in front of them. Finally, Tree Frog spoke again.

"After the fight, Carrier," he said, "let's smoke again, you and me."

"All right, my friend. We will."

Carrier wanted to talk about Potmaker, but somehow the time didn't seem right, and Tree Frog's last remark had sounded as if it had been meant to be the concluding statement of the conversation. Carrier stood up to leave while Tree Frog gathered up his little bundle of belongings, which included his pipe and tobacco. Both men went inside the townhouse where they would sleep. As Carrier stretched out for the night, he thought about Tree Frog's last statement and about his own cheerful response. And he wondered if they would be able to live up to that agreement.

They marched all together at first. They stayed together as far as the burned-out village. There they stopped and held a final, quick council. Then Tree Frog led fifty men on down the road, but well before they would reach the occupied village, he would lead them off into the forest. They would circle the village widely to avoid being detected by the enemy, and then they would position themselves for an attack on the village from the west. There they would wait.

The others held back until Tree Frog's group was well out of sight. Then He-Fights-with-Alligators took half the Calusas and followed, but they would not go as far through the forest as had Tree Frog's group. When they found themselves directly north of the village and still hidden in the forest, they would position themselves for attack and wait.

Creeping Panther and the rest of the Calusas, with Potmaker for a guide, for she had insisted on taking part in the fight, left at the same time, but when the first group of Calusas left the trail to circle north, this group headed south. They would locate themselves in the forest just south of the village, just opposite the group led by He-Fights-with-Alligators, and there they would wait.

That left Big Conch and his main force of Timucuas still on

the road to the east of the occupied village. Big Conch, with his followers, would wait patiently until he knew that the other three groups had been given enough time to get themselves into position. Then he would start the attack from the east. As soon as the other three groups heard the sounds of his attack, they would join in, and the hated white men would be subjected to a fierce surprise attack from all sides at once by a large force. This was the plan that Big Conch and the others had laid the night before.

Carrier waited with Big Conch, and he found his palms perspiring with anxiety. He was ready for the fight. He had been ready for some time. It was hard for him to wait longer, but of course, he knew that he must. The plan was a good one, and if anything would work, he told himself, this would.

He wished that he had gone with the group that included Potmaker, for he hated to be separated from her, especially in time of danger. The last time she had been involved in a fight with the *Ani-'squani*, she had been captured. He wondered if he would be able to spot her in the heat of battle, and then he wondered if he should even try. He should concentrate on the fight. He knew that.

He only hoped that she would do the same and take care of her own safety. He was already looking forward to the talk he would have with her after the big fight.

Eighteen

T HE TIME has been long enough," Big Conch said. "Let's go to the village. Let's go fight."

Without waiting for any response, he started down the road toward the occupied village at a quick trot. Carrier was right beside him and had to hold himself back to keep from running out ahead. His heart was racing and pounding, but not because of the pace. He was anxious for the fight. He wanted to be in the middle of it, and now it was just ahead.

They had gone about half the distance to the village when Big Conch picked up the pace, and Carrier's spirits lifted. Still, he wanted to go even faster. His arm ached to deal the first blow. Then the village loomed suddenly ahead, and Big Conch raced toward it as fast as he could, brandishing his warclub high over his head, and Carrier raced along with him.

They ran on, and then Carrier could actually see the white men in the village ahead. He was amazed that they seemed to be unaware of the fifty or so men racing toward them waving weapons, ready for the kill. Then one of the white men looked up and in their direction and saw them. He yelled out something, a startled warning of some kind, and almost immediately, Big Conch allowed a waiting war whoop to burst from his lungs. Carrier, in the manner of his own people, the Real People, gobbled like a turkey.

Just then the men to the rear stopped running and released a shower of arrows into the village over the heads of their comrades. From the west, Tree Frog's group did the same. White men in the village screamed, ducked and ran for shelter. Several were hit, but none were killed. At the same time, the big beasts that He-Fights-with-Alligators had called caballos were stamping around and screaming with pain, for a number of them had also been hit by the arrows.

Then the attackers were coming into the village from all directions. Big Conch came first upon a fallen white man with an arrow in his thigh. He bashed the hairy-faced man on the head with his heavy warclub and crushed the skull. Then he looked around for the next closest enemy.

As Carrier raced into the village, a big white man with a long knife in his hand raced to meet him, shouting angry but unintelligible words. Carrier braced himself. The man came close and swung the long knife, but Carrier managed to duck under the blade just in time. From his crouched position, he swung his own warclub upward between the man's legs, delivering a crushing blow to the crotch. The man screamed and doubled over, dropping his long knife. Carrier pushed the man backward, picked up the long knife and thrust it into the man's chest. He pulled it out again and brandished it in his right hand, looking around for someone else on whom to use the remarkable weapon.

A white man stepped out of one of the houses and aimed a fire stick. The stick barked and belched flames, and a Timucua just to the right of Carrier screamed and fell, his side all bloody from the bits of metal flung by the stick.

Carrier raced ahead and swung the big knife at the shooter, slicing it into the man's arm. The man roared in pain, dropped the shooting stick and reached awkwardly with his good arm for a short knife at his belt. Carrier stabbed him in the belly with the long knife. Instinctively the man grabbed at the blade, and as Carrier pulled it back out, the man's hands were sliced open. For an instant, Carrier looked into the man's face, and the man returned his gaze. The watery eyes were wide, and the mouth was hanging open. Carrier was about to stab again when the man pitched forward to lie still on the ground. Carrier turned to look elsewhere for a fight.

Then some of the attackers from the north and from the west began setting fire to the houses, and soon the flames were roaring, adding more confusion to the shouts and screams and groans of the battle. Some attackers still held back some distance and fired arrows when they could get good, clean shots at the white men.

A *'squani* came running out of a burning house, his clothing ablaze. Carrier started to attack him with the long knife, but changed his mind.

"No," he told himself. "Let him burn."

To his left and a little forward he saw Big Conch engaged in a fierce, hand-to-hand struggle with a hairy, stocky man. They fell to the ground and rolled over and over before the white man wound up on top with the advantage. His hands were around the throat of Big Conch, and the Timucua's hands were on the other's wrists trying to pry loose their grip. Carrier ran over to where the combatants struggled and slid the long blade into the white man's back, pushing it all the way through. The white man shuddered and fell forward. Carrier pulled the blade free, and Big Conch shoved the body to one side and jumped to his feet, ready to meet another enemy.

At the opposite end of the village, He-Fights-with-Alligators faced an Español armed with a long lance. Both men paused, recognition and hatred on their faces.

"*¡Tu! ¡Bastardo!*" said the Español through his teeth.

"*Tu diablo,*" said He-Fights-with-Alligators. "*Hijo de perra.*"

They were standing too close together for an effective thrust with the long lance, so the white man raised it up over his head to use it like a club. The Calusa ducked and ran headlong into the man's midsection, carrying him back and down onto the ground. They landed hard with a thud, and a cloud of dust rose around them.

He-Fights-with-Alligators pulled the flint knife out of the sheath at his waist and thrust hard, but it glanced off a rib, tearing an ugly gash along the Español's side and exposing part of the white bone. The hated Español screamed in enraged pain and struggled to get out from under the Calusa. He-Fights-with-Alligators struck again, and this time the flint blade went deep into the other man's chest, just under the sternum. Blood spewed forth, soaking the Calusa's right arm from the elbow down.

Another white man stepped up behind He-Fights-with-Alligators, who was still straddling the dying man's torso, and drew out his long knife to strike, but before he had raised it over his head, an arrow embedded itself between his shoulder blades with a sickening thud. He stood almost motionless for a moment, a startled expression on his face, and, as He-Fights-with-Alligators stood up and turned to face the man, he fell forward dead.

. . . .

Potmaker ran up and down the southern edge of the village with a flaming brand in her hand, lighting houses as she went. Just as she torched one, a white man with a long knife in his hand stepped around the corner to face her. She recognized him. She knew him. She hated him. As he raised his arm to strike, she shoved the torch into the man's face. He roared in astonishment and horror, dropped his long knife and clawed at his face with both hands, but it was too late. His nose was broken and bloody, and his face hair was already burning. As he staggered forward blindly, Potmaker beat him several times on the head with the torch until he dropped to his knees.

Carrier looked in that direction just in time to see the last two blows. He was proud, and he knew even more than before that he wanted that woman for his own. He also knew that he could not afford to stand and watch her, so he turned to get back into the fight. She would take care of herself, he told himself. She would do all right.

The battle raged on. A few archers still loosed occasional arrows, and every now and then a white man fired one of the fire sticks, but mostly it was warclubs and long lances and knives both short and long. It was stabbing, bludgeoning and strangling. The air was filled with the smell of smoke and of blood and guts and the sounds of screaming and groaning, of shouted angry words and of blows and of stamping feet.

Tree Frog had beaten down three of the enemy with his warclub. His chest was covered with blood, but not his own. He had just crushed the skull of the third and was surveying the battleground looking for another victim. He was standing in front of a burning house, just a short distance away. He-Fights-with-Alligators was running past to get back into the fight, and he glanced in Tree Frog's direction. Suddenly he stopped.

"Tree Frog," he called out. "Get away from that house."

He had seen the barrels of black powder inside, and he knew that the flames would get to them soon, perhaps they had already, and the explosion could come anytime. But Tree Frog did not know about the black powder. How could he tell him? How could he warn him in time?

"Tree Frog. Get away. Get away."

Tree Frog then realized that the Calusa was calling his name, but he had not understood the rest of what he had said. There was too much noise in the air and too much confusion. He looked at He-Fights-with-Alligators with a questioning look. Then the powder exploded.

The roar was deafening, and the impact was tremendous. The Timucuas and their allies had never seen or heard anything like it before. They ran from the village into the forest in all directions. If they had their hands on the throat of an enemy, they dropped him and ran. The flames spewed, the smoke bellowed and the air was filled with flying and falling debris and with a sickening, acrid odor. They ran. They ran, but Tree Frog did not run with them. Tree Frog never knew what hit him. He was dead, and the battle was over.

He-Fights-with-Alligators did not run far. He ran into the forest and returned to the place from which he had watched the Españols for so much time before, and again he watched.

Garay stepped out into the center of the village and surveyed the carnage around him. The casualties on both sides had been heavy. All around men groaned. Garay began yelling orders, and the men at last responded. Some started to tend to the wounded. Others lined up the bodies of their own dead to count them and to prepare them for burial.

No one bothered to try to put out the fires. They were already beyond control. The village was a total loss. He-Fights-with-Alligators wondered what the Españols would do next. Would they regroup and move inland? Look for another village to occupy? He watched as one man, in response to an order from Garay, made his way to where the caballos had been kept, and he saw that only a few seemed to be unhurt.

Soon the men began to pick up what could be salvaged from the ruins. Mostly it was weapons. They picked some armor out of the ashes of the burned houses. Some tools and other equipment which had been outside when the attack came were unharmed. Not much, though, had escaped the flames.

He-Fights-with-Alligators continued to watch as the men gathered up what was left of their belongings. Two of the men went to the caballos. They slit the throats of those that were badly wounded, and they gathered the lead ropes of the few remaining healthy ones. Other men were digging holes in the ground where the bodies had been lined up.

As He-Fights-with-Alligators watched, Garay walked over to where the men were digging. He looked at the holes in the ground, waited for a short while impatiently and then said something which the hidden Calusa could not hear clearly. The men quit digging and unceremoniously dumped the bodies of their dead companions into the holes. Then they began to put the dirt back in on top of the bodies.

In a short while they were done, and Garay barked another command. A man brought him his caballo with a saddle on its back, and Garay climbed aboard. He started riding toward the west, toward the coast, toward where his big boats waited in the water. The others all followed him on foot in single file. Some led the few remaining caballos with bundles hastily loaded on their backs. The others each carried something of the salvaged equipment. They all walked toward the water.

He-Fights-with-Alligators followed them, keeping well hidden in the forest, moving slowly and cautiously, not yet quite daring to believe what was happening. He followed until there was no more forest cover, and he lurked there and watched as the Españols huddled there at the water's edge.

Someone shouted toward the boats. He had to shout several times before he got a response. Then the men on one of the big boats lowered small boats into the water and rowed them ashore. The survivors of the bloody fight, all of them, including Francisco de Garay himself, climbed into the small boats and were rowed back out to the waiting big boats.

They all climbed aboard, leaving the caballos behind. He-Fights-with-Alligators wondered why they did not bother to load the caballos. Perhaps, he decided, they were in too big a hurry to get away to bother with the beasts. Soon the big boats were sailing away. The Españols had been defeated. They were leaving. All of them. It was over—this time.

Nineteen

DANCING RABBIT had at last discarded his crutch. He limped somewhat grotesquely around Kituwah with the aid of a walking stick, also fashioned especially for him by Doya. It was becoming more and more obvious to Dancing Rabbit that his traveling days were over, and now and then he became angry at himself for the foolish accident that had brought him to this sad state. It was as if he had become an old man before his time.

But most of the time he felt good that he no longer had to hobble on a crutch. He felt much more mobile with the walking stick, in spite of his limp. However, his mood was darkened some because he was beginning to worry about his nephew Carrier.

Carrier was now, according to Dancing Rabbit's calculations, long overdue. Dancing Rabbit had said nothing about his worries to his sister Walnut, for he didn't want to worry her unnecessarily, but one afternoon, just as Dancing Rabbit was finishing up the bowl of soup his sister had prepared for him, she brought the subject up herself. He had been afraid that she might.

"It's been a long time now since my son left for the south," she said.

"It's a long journey," said Dancing Rabbit. "And before he starts the return trip, there's much trading to be done. Perhaps he's taken some time to rest in between. Maybe he even went farther south, down to the country of the *Ani-Calusa.*"

"I think it's been too long. When you made the same trip before, it didn't take so long as this time."

"But I had Carrier with me to help me with things. He's alone. He has no help. It could be that's what's taking him longer. We were two. He's just one."

"I know," she said. "That worries me too. What if he's run into some kind of trouble? He's all alone."

"He can take care of himself," said Dancing Rabbit. "He's young and strong and smart. He'll be all right."

"Yes," said Walnut. "I suppose so."

But Dancing Rabbit could tell by the tone of her voice that he had not convinced her, that she didn't really "suppose so." And, of course, he couldn't blame her. He wasn't even convinced himself. He was worried. It had been too long. He knew that. Along the way were *Ani-Cusa* and *Ani-Chahta*, sometime enemies of the Real People. And, of course, there were other dangers.

Dancing Rabbit wondered about the stories of the strange men from across the sea, the men with white skin and hairy faces who rode across the land on great four-legged beasts, who had weapons like no one had ever before seen, who supposedly slaughtered people brutally and casually. He wondered if the stories about these men might be true. What if they were, and what if those people were down there in the land of the Timucuas where Carrier had gone to trade?

Dancing Rabbit tried to put all those thoughts out of his mind. It was no use, he told himself, thinking the worst when one had no way of knowing what really was happening—or had already happened and was over and done. True, Wasulu had indicated that everything would be all right. Yet he worried. If only he still had two good legs, he thought, he would start south immediately and search for his nephew.

And Dancing Rabbit had another worry, a secret one, one he could not share with anyone else. If anything had happened to the young man, Dancing Rabbit thought, he would have to search for another young man to whom to teach the writing. And he could think of no one else he would be able to trust the way he trusted his nephew. He felt a little guilty for this last worry. It seemed somehow selfish, even though he told himself that the writing was important.

One of his greatest fears, perhaps his single greatest fear, was that the writing might die with him. It was very sacred, the writing, and he felt that it must survive. There would come a day, someday, when the excesses of the *Ani-Kutani* would be forgotten. Then whoever knew the writing would be able to make it known again. It had to survive.

Dancing Rabbit got up from his seat with the help of his walking stick and took leave of his sister. He walked for a while aimlessly around the town, but soon he found himself at the gateway. He stood for a moment. Then he walked between the walls and out of the town. He continued a short distance down the road until he came to a small mound off to his right, a kind of smooth hump in the ground. He moved over to the mound and sat down on it, and he stared off toward the south, longing for the sight of his nephew coming home.

Then the thought came into Dancing Rabbit's mind that he was sitting there on the very mound where, years before, the boy Gnat had sat determinedly waiting for his uncle to return from the West when everyone else had given him up for dead. Well, now the boy was grown, and the man was old and crippled, and the man sat there in the same spot waiting for the boy. He wondered if he would have as much patience and determination as had the boy Gnat. He wondered also if his vigil would be rewarded, as the boy's had been.

He had not rested there long when a rabbit popped up just across the road from him. It sat up straight and seemed to be looking right at him deliberately.

" '*Siyo*, Jisdu," said Dancing Rabbit. "What brings you here?"

He had not thought for some time about his seeming special relationship to the curious little creature, the trickster of the tales of the Real People, but suddenly he felt as if the rabbit had come to him on purpose for some special reason. He almost expected it to answer his question, but it did not. Instead it sat still, staring at him with its split nose twitching.

"I haven't seen you for a long time, Jisdu, my friend," said Dancing Rabbit. "Have you come to tell me something?"

Then the rabbit's ears gave a forward twitch, and it seemed to vault sideways, and it quickly disappeared from Dancing Rabbit's view. Dancing Rabbit stared after it with intense curiosity. He even had an urge to try to follow the little creature, but he resisted the urge. Besides, he knew that he would not be able to keep up with it, especially with his crippled leg.

"Did he come to see me?" he asked himself. "If so, to what end? He told me nothing. Or did he? Each time in the past when Jisdu came to me, everything worked out well in the end. And I didn't understand him those times either. Not until later. Perhaps that is what he told me this time. That everything will be all right after all. Perhaps."

Still he sat and he watched, and he did not go back inside

the walls of Kituwah to the house of his sister until the sun was low in the western sky.

Early the next morning, Dancing Rabbit limped to the home of White Tobacco. He had already received assurances from Wasulu, but in matters of grave importance, he thought, one could never be sure enough. He found the old man sitting alone beneath the arbor which stood beside his house.

" '*Siyo*, Uncle," said Dancing Rabbit.

" '*Siyo. Tohiju?*"

"*Osd'. Nihina?*"

"Oh, I'm not doing so badly for an old man," said the conjurer. "Come in and sit down with me. We'll smoke together."

"*Wado*," said Dancing Rabbit, and he walked under the arbor and took a seat on the bench across from White Tobacco. A small fire burned on the ground between them. White Tobacco picked up a short clay pipe and filled its bowl from a pouch. Then he lit it with a faggot from the fire. He puffed a few times to get the tobacco in the bowl burning, and clouds of blue-gray smoke obscured his wrinkled face from Dancing Rabbit's vision. In a moment, the old man passed the pipe to Dancing Rabbit, who took it and puffed four times, then returned it.

"I'm worried about my nephew Carrier," he said. "He's been gone a long time now. Longer than the trip should take. His mother's worried too. I tried to tell her reasons the trip might be taking longer this time, but I don't think it helped. Besides, I'm worried too, even though I tried not to let her know."

"There are many dangers along the way," said White Tobacco. "Especially for a young man alone."

"Yes," said Dancing Rabbit. "I know," and he felt a pang of

guilt for having approved of the trip in the first place. He had known at the time that his sister did not approve, and he had persuaded her to let the boy go.

White Tobacco took another puff on the pipe and handed it again to Dancing Rabbit. Dancing Rabbit smoked in silence, wondering what the old man might do. He handed the pipe back again, and the old man finished it and put it away. Then he found another pouch from which he produced two small, round beads, one black, the other red.

He took the black bead in his left hand and the red in his right, and he held them loosely in a peculiar manner between his thumb and index finger. His elbows rested on his knees, and he leaned forward and seemed to be studying the beads intently. Dancing Rabbit too strained to see.

The old man's hands were remarkably still and steady, yet, suddenly, the black bead in the left hand seemed to move, just a little, along the index finger. It seemed to move of its own volition. And Dancing Rabbit felt a sudden pang of cold fear.

Then the black bead was still again, and in the right hand the red bead moved. It moved clearly and unmistakably along the still index finger, and the old man smiled. Dancing Rabbit breathed a sigh of relief. The chill of the black bead left him, yet still he waited anxiously for a soothing word from White Tobacco. The old man put the beads back into the pouch.

"I think that your nephew has had some trouble there in the south," he said, "but I think that it's over. I think that he will come home safely. Even so, maybe we should do what we can to help the rest of his journey."

"Yes," said Dancing Rabbit. "I think that would be good."

White Tobacco stood up and moved to the back of the arbor. There, with a loud groan, he squatted down on his haunches. A variety of baskets, bundles and bowls were lined up there. He found a small empty bowl, and then he took a handful of tobacco out of a larger bowl and put it into the small one. From other bowls he took out a pinch or two of whatever was in them and dropped it in with the tobacco. Then he picked up a stick and began to stir the mixture in the small bowl, and Dancing Rabbit thought that he could hear the old man singing in a very low and quiet voice.

Finished, the old man poured the mixture out of the bowl onto a small skin, wrapped it up and tied it. He stood up, slowly and with some effort, and turned to hand the small bundle to Dancing Rabbit.

"Smoke this," he said, "four times a day. Blow the smoke toward the south."

Dancing Rabbit accepted the pouch.

"Yes," he said. "I will. *Wado.*"

Back at his sister's house, Dancing Rabbit was in better spirits than when he had left. He smiled as he greeted Walnut, and he sat down in a corner of the house with a groan. His leg was hurting, and he was tired. It had been a long day, and he had walked more than usual, but, he thought, it had been well worth the effort. He would gladly do it again and more.

"Sister," he said, a wide smile on his pumpkin-like face, "I think that everything will be all right now. I think you don't have to worry about my nephew."

She gave him a questioning look, and he seemed so smug that her expression almost changed to anger. She saw the small bundle he had brought home with him, but she did not question him, not beyond the look she had given him, and he did not volunteer anything more. She knew though that he must have some reason, and probably a good one, for his changed mood and for the statement he had made, and she had a pretty good idea of what might be in the bundle and where it had probably come from.

"*Agiyosi,*" he said. "Do you have anything for me to eat?"

Dancing Rabbit felt better than he had felt for some days. Jisdu had appeared to him to give him encouragement, and White Tobacco had looked into the future with his beads and predicted success. Then just to make doubly sure, the old man had prepared some special tobacco for Dancing Rabbit to smoke to ensure the safe return of Carrier. Everything was positive. Everything looked good.

The following morning with the first appearance of the sun, Dancing Rabbit smoked the special blend, and he blew the smoke toward the south. He smoked it again later in the morning and then again about mid-afternoon. It made him feel as if he was helping his nephew even though he was unable to travel to his aid. Then early in the evening, he smoked again, but this time he smoked on the small mound outside of town, and when he was done, he sat down once again on the mound, staring off toward the south, and there he watched and waited.

Twenty

AT THE VILLAGE of Big Conch, there was a great victory celebration. It was possibly the biggest victory celebration the people had ever staged, for certainly the victory over the invading white men was the biggest victory in the memories of any of the people there. There were dancing and singing long into the night, and there was much formal boasting of deeds done in battle.

But as soon as the victory celebration was concluded, there followed several days of mourning for the dead and purification rites for those who had taken part in the fight. He-Fights-with-Alligators, his uncle Creeping Panther and the rest of the Calusas stayed with the Timucuas for all that time and took part in the Timucua ceremonies. So did Carrier.

Then, with things more or less back to normal in the village of Big Conch and the land of the Timucuas in general, the Calusas announced their intention to return to their own homes. He-Fights-with-Alligators was anxiously longing, yearning, to be reunited with his wife, since he had learned that she had been waiting for him all the long time of his absence, and Creeping Panther reminded everyone that there were also Calusa dead. Their relatives back home would still have to be notified, and there would be a time of mourning there as well.

Gifts were heaped on the Calusas, and there were exchanged pledges of eternal friendship and gratitude. But there was also an ominous note to all of these proceedings injected by the one man among them who knew the strangers best.

"These Españols," said He-Fights-with-Alligators, "these white men, sooner or later will come back. All of us, Calusas, Timucuas, even our Chiloki friends to the north, will have to be watchful from now on. I have lived with those men. They are brutal beyond belief, and there are many of them. Their big boats keep bringing more of them from across the waters. They have weapons that we don't have, and their weapons are superior to ours. They have their big boats and their big beasts. They have the black powder that explodes. We defeated them this time, but there will be other times and other white men. We have to be watchful and stay ready for them whenever they might appear."

Then the Calusas left, carrying with them their bundles of gifts, their newly acquired war honors and the sadness of the loss of some of their numbers.

During all this time, Carrier had scarcely spoken to Potmaker, for she had been one of the many mourners. She had lost her brother, and as far as Carrier could tell, that loss had left her alone among her own people. The Timucuas, he thought, must have clans just as did the Real People, and if so, she would have clan relatives somewhere. But there did not appear to be any close relatives. He had not heard Potmaker or Tree Frog speak of parents or uncles or other brothers or sisters.

She seemed to be alone, and he longed for a time to speak with her alone so as to resume the conversation he had initiated before the big fight, the conversation that she had promised to continue later.

He had also begun to think about his own return to Kituwah. He would arrive back home as a trader with nothing to show from his trip, nothing but the one long knife he had taken during the battle. His first journey alone, a journey he had begun with such confidence and high hopes, had turned out to be a total failure. He wondered what his uncle and his mother would think of him. What would the people of Kituwah and the other towns nearby say when they found out?

"If Dancing Rabbit had been able to go, it would not have been this way."

He could almost hear the voices. Yet he was anxious to get home and to begin to gather the wares for another trip. He would not quit on a failure. And, he thought, the reaction to his failure might be somewhat tempered by reaction to the news he would bring, news of the existence of the strangers and of the fights that he had taken part in. So in spite of his disappointment and his anxiety concerning the reaction of his people, yet he was ready to begin the long journey home.

Then at last the mourning time was done, and Carrier went to seek out Potmaker. It didn't take him long, for there were few places to look. He found her sitting alone on the bank of a nearby creek, just sitting there, watching the water run by. Carrier wondered if Potmaker's people, the Timucuas, like his own, listened to the running water hoping to hear its messages. He stood still, waiting for her to take notice of his presence. And at last she did. She looked up at him. Still he stood in silence waiting for her to say the first word, waiting to be invited to stay so he would not be thought an intruder into her privacy.

"Carrier," she said, and she smiled a soft, sad smile. "Come and sit with me."

Carrier sat down beside her and stared into the running water. It was swift-running, clear and clean, and the sound it made as it ran over its rocky bed was pleasant to hear.

"Is it time yet for us to finish our talk?" he asked her.

"Yes," she said. "It's time enough. We can talk now."

"I'm going home soon," he said. "I want you to go with me back to my people. I want you to stay with me there and be my wife."

"I don't know," she said.

"Is there some man you're thinking about here among your own people?"

"No. It isn't that."

"I know that a man should live with his wife's people. But I cannot stay here. I have to go back home."

He was thinking of the writing and of his pledge to his uncle to keep it alive, though secret. There were many reasons he wanted to go back home, but that was the one reason he must do so.

"Oh, that's all right," said Potmaker. "I don't have any more close relatives here anyway, and my own village has been destroyed, my own home. I guess I really have no home now. I would gladly go with you to your people, Carrier, except—"

She stopped, and Carrier waited for her to continue, but she did not. She said no more, and the silence became awkward. Carrier reached out and put a hand on Potmaker's shoulder, and he felt that touch throughout his body. It surprised him, and it was a wonderful feeling, and it made him long for more. He left his hand resting there on her cool skin.

"What?" he said. "You said you would gladly go with me. Except for what?"

"Carrier," she said, "you know that the white men captured me."

"Of course I know that. When they made me go for the Calusas instead of staying here to help you, I felt bad. I wanted to go for you right away, but they all thought that it would be better if I went for the Calusas. They promised me that they would get you out of there."

"And they were right about all of that. That's not what I'm talking about."

"Then what?" he asked.

"You don't know what those men did with me while I was their captive," she said, and she turned her face away from him.

He paused a moment before answering her. His jaws tightened. The hatred for the *Ani-'squani* welled up again inside him.

"I know," he said. "It's what they would do, and I hate them for it. I thought about it when I killed them, but what they did has nothing to do with the way I feel about you."

"Not even if I were to have a little one because of them?"

"A little one?" said Carrier. He stared into the water for a moment in silence. Potmaker still looked away from him. "You can't know that already?" he added. "Can you? So soon?"

"No," she said. "It is too soon. But I have a feeling. I can't explain it any more than that. I might be wrong, but it could happen."

"Yes," he said. "It could, I guess. And if it does happen, what would you do with it, with the little one?"

"I don't know. It would be mine. I might decide to keep it

and raise it. What would you think about that? How would it make you feel? Would you want me even then?"

"Yes," said Carrier. "I would. I do want you. More than ever. And if what you think may happen should really happen, then whatever you decide to do about it will be all right with me. Now will you go with me?"

At last Potmaker turned and looked Carrier in the face, and she smiled.

"Yes," she said. "I will."

Carrier and Potmaker went back into the village and walked together to the house of Big Conch. As they approached the house, Big Conch saw them coming, and he stepped out to meet them, a broad smile on his face.

"I've been looking for you, trader," he said.

"We came to see you," said Carrier, "but I guess I'm not a trader any longer. My goods are all lost."

"Yes," said Big Conch, and he laughed. "That's what I want to talk to you about. But first, why did you come to see me?"

Carrier looked at Potmaker, standing there beside him, and he put an arm around her shoulders.

"I'm taking this woman back home with me," he said, "to be my wife."

Big Conch looked at Potmaker, and she smiled and ducked her head somewhat demurely. Big Conch laughed again, and Carrier thought that it was good to hear laughter once more.

"That's good," said Big Conch. "I'm happy for you both. Something good should come out of these bad times. Now listen to me. My nephew has found something interesting. I want to show it to you."

Carrier looked toward Big Conch with curiosity, but all he could detect was the broad grin. It was as if Big Conch was about to play a big joke.

"Yes?" said Carrier.

"Hey," Big Conch shouted, turning his head slightly to call over his shoulder. "Nephew. Bring that thing out here."

A young man came out of the house of Big Conch dragging a large bundle. Carrier recognized it immediately. It was the bundle of trade goods he had hidden when he had first realized that the *Ani-'squani* were nearby.

"My goods," he said. "Where did you find them?"

"Near the big water," said the nephew. "Just in the forest at the edge of the beach."

"Just where I hid them," said Carrier. "After all that has happened, I was sure that the white men had found them. I didn't even think of going back to look for them."

"So let's trade, trader," said Big Conch, his grin broader than ever.

When Carrier unwrapped his bundle, he found that everything was there and nothing was broken. He spread his wares, and the people of the village came with their own goods to exchange. But they didn't haggle with him at all. They took what they wanted of what he had to offer, and they gave him more than what he asked in return. They were trading. Yes. But they were giving gifts as well, without calling them gifts.

He had more than he had hoped for. He had abundant shells of every shape and color, some of the best he had ever seen. He had chunks of salt and slabs of dried fish and pearls from the oyster beds. And there were other things as well: herbs and fruits and nuts from that southern country, and bright, colorful feathers from various birds that lived in those parts, feathers of every imaginable color.

And finally he had a pile of goods which some of the people had salvaged and cleaned up as best they could from the ashes of the burnt village, the site of the big battle, things the white men had left behind. There were several knives, both short and long. There was a shield and a helmet and a breastplate. There was even a part of one of the fire sticks which the white men used to shoot bits of metal through the air. Carrier had more, much more, to take home than he had brought down.

"My friend," said Big Conch, "do you think you've done well enough, or will you be ashamed to return home with so little to show for your trip?"

"I have so much here," said Carrier, "that I don't know if I'll be able to carry it all back."

"Oh, well then," said Big Conch, "you must have a boat to load it in."

He nodded toward his nephew, who grinned and ran around behind the house. Soon he reappeared with a friend. The two of them were carrying a long, lightweight canoe made of cypress wood.

"This is for you," said the nephew.

"Thank you, my friends," said Carrier. "This has been a good trading trip for me."

"You came by land," said Big Conch. "Do you know the water way back to your country?"

"I've not traveled it before," said Carrier, "but I think I can find my way."

"It will be much easier, though, with someone who has gone that way before. My brother-in-law has traveled it. He and his son, my nephew here, will go with you."

"Thank you, my friends," said Carrier. "I won't forget my Timucua friends. We'll be leaving in the morning."

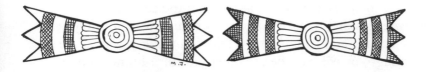

Twenty-one

CARRIER and his new traveling companions were met just outside of Kituwah with much enthusiasm and joy. Many there had already decided that they would probably never see Carrier again. So when Dancing Rabbit, who had been sitting on the mound of earth keeping his lonely vigil just outside of the town, had seen the four people approaching, had stood up anxiously to watch, squinting his eyes at the figures until he had recognized his nephew among them and knew there was no mistake, ran toward the town walls shouting, "Carrier's coming. Carrier's coming," many of the people ran out of the town to meet him.

Carrier felt good. His chest swelled a bit, and he picked up the pace some. He saw his uncle there and heard him call out to the town. Then he saw the people starting to come out to meet him. He had with him the woman he wanted for his wife and two good friends and traveling companions. He had a load of trade goods much more valuable than anything he had originally expected to return home with.

Then it began to look as though the entire town had rushed out from behind the walls to greet him. When the noise of the initial excitement died down enough for him to be heard, Dancing Rabbit announced that everyone should go back inside the walls and gather at the townhouse to hear Carrier's tale. The people turned and rushed back in to follow Dancing Rabbit's advice, while the wily Dancing Rabbit, with his sister Walnut, deliberately lagged behind the others to walk back more slowly into town with his nephew and the other newcomers.

"Uncle, Mother," said Carrier, "this is Potmaker of the Timucuas. She is going to be my wife. And these are my good Timucua friends, Dark Panther and He-Goes-at-Night."

He spoke to his uncle in the trade language so that the Timucuas could understand what was being said, and then, because his mother did not understand that jargon, he repeated it in the language of the Real People.

"This is my uncle, Dancing Rabbit, and this is my mother, Walnut," he added for the benefit of the Timucuas, again speaking the jargon.

They walked together, Dancing Rabbit limping along in the lead, and made their way to the townhouse. Then Dancing Rabbit practically shoved Carrier to a place in front of the crowd.

"Are you ready to talk to the people?" he asked.

"Yes."

Carrier told the people the whole tale, how he had encountered the *Ani-Cusa* on his trip to the south, how the Apalachees had warned him of the white men, whom he called *Ani-'squani*, how when he finally arrived at the Timucua village that had been his goal, he had found it occupied by the *Ani-'squani*, and how they had chased him into the forest.

He told about his hiding of his wares and meeting the Calusa, He-Fights-with-Alligators, in the forest. He described the fights with the white men, and then he told how the Timucuas had recovered his wares for him and traded with him at last. And he told the entire population that Potmaker was to be his wife. When he had finished, some of the people began to ask him questions.

"So these strangers we've heard so many rumors about really do exist," someone said.

"They exist, and they are as bad as anything you've heard about them," said Carrier. "They are vicious, brutal people who try to kill or to take captive anyone they meet. The Calusa I told you about before, He-Fights-with-Alligators, had been their slave for a long time, several years, I think."

"Do they really have white skin and hair on their faces?"

"Yes. That's all true. And their hair comes in many different colors. Some of them have black hair like ours, but others have brown hair or red or yellow."

"Do they really ride on the backs of big animals? Is that true too?"

"Yes. The beasts are like deer, but much larger, and they have no antlers. The *Ani-'squani* put leather seats on the backs of the animals and ride on them, or they tie their bundles on the backs of the animals to carry."

"We've heard that these strangers— What did you call them?"

"*Ani-Asquani,*" said Carrier. "That's what the Calusa who speaks their language called them."

"We've heard that these—*Ani-'squani* have powerful weapons like nothing we've ever seen before. Tell us about their weapons."

Carrier began to untie his bundles of wares. He produced a breastplate, held it up before him to show its purpose, then tossed it on the ground before the crowd. They were startled by the sound it made when it hit the ground. Then they touched it, rubbed it to feel its strange texture, thumped it to hear the sound and to test its hardness, and passed it around, marveling at the strange metal. Then Carrier pulled out a short knife and passed it around. There was more amazement than before.

But the people were really astonished at the long knife. Carrier hacked into a log with it to show both its hardness and its sharpness. Finally he showed them the shooting tube or fire stick. He explained to them that it had been in a fire and its wooden handle was missing, and he told them how it exploded and shot bits of metal out of its tube. He also told them about the black powder and tried his best to impress upon them the power of the explosion of the kegs of powder that had ended the big fight.

"These are truly wonderful things," he heard someone say, and of course he understood the reaction. He had thought like that himself not so long ago. Yet the remark worried him for some reason. He stepped back and allowed the people to continue to marvel among themselves at the things he had brought back, to satisfy their curiosity, and when they had begun to quiet down again, and to look toward him for more information, he spoke to them once more.

"It's true," he said, "that these strange invaders have brought with them many wonderful things. That was my own thought when I went to the land of the Timucuas, and I had heard before that the strangers might be there. I hoped that they would be there. I hoped that I might see them and meet them so that I might trade with them for some of their goods.

"I did see them, and I did manage to bring some of their things back here with me. But I wish I had never seen them, and I hope that I never see them again.

"These things, as wonderful as they are, are not worth the

pain and suffering the *Ani-'squani* bring with them. I think that we should keep a watch for their approach at all times."

He was echoing the words of He-Fights-with-Alligators. He knew it. It was conscious imitation. It was the best advice he could think of. Yet he knew that these people would not really believe him. No one could believe the descriptions of the *Ani-'squani*. He remembered his own early skepticism, and then his own horror when he had actually encountered them. One really had to see them to believe the tales. Still he had to try.

"If ever we see them coming our way or hear that they are coming in this direction, hide everything of value, and then hide yourselves. Let them find nothing of any value. Let them come across empty towns. Hide and wait for them to go away."

"But you defeated them. You drove them away, those you didn't kill."

"Yes," said Carrier, "but there were many lives lost on both sides. And we had the help of Calusa allies. We surprised them and overwhelmed them with numbers."

"Do you think they'll come again?"

"Will they come to our country, do you think?"

"I don't know," said Carrier, "but the Calusa who had been their captive and had learned their language and their ways said that there are many of them. He said the big boats keep coming, bringing more and more of them. He said that we should all be watchful, and I think that he was right. I think that his advice was good."

There was a feast that night. There were singing and dancing, and everyone ate more than his fill. The visitors, including Potmaker, were given places to sleep in the townhouse, but not until Walnut, with the help of translations from her brother, had assured her future daughter-in-law that she would help her build her own house, starting the very next day. Since Potmaker was not one of the Real People and therefore had no clan among them, the house would be built near her own, she said. The long night was almost over before anyone stopped celebrating and crawled into bed to sleep.

The next day started late, and what was left of it was given over to more trading of goods, to the spreading around of the newly acquired wealth. Some of the wares were owed in payment to local people whose own goods Carrier had taken south. While this was going on, Potmaker and Walnut were already building the new house. The Timucua guests were visiting, telling various inhabitants more tales of the recent battles with the white men and of the trip back north.

It had been rather uneventful, they said. Carrier had been very clever at avoiding any contact with any potential enemies along the way. The goods with which he had returned and the tales of what had happened in the south were rapidly making Carrier into a new hero.

When at last he found his opportunity, Dancing Rabbit got his nephew alone for a talk.

"I'm proud of you, nephew," he said. "For a while, we worried. We were afraid that we wouldn't see you again. But here you are, and you've had a very good trip. You've done better this time than the two of us ever did together."

"It wasn't because of my trading skills, Uncle," said Carrier. "It was because I fought with them against the invaders that the Timucuas gave me so much in exchange for my own goods."

"Whatever the reason, you brought it all back, and from all the reports, you handled yourself well in a very difficult time.

Ah, but I'm glad that you're back here with us now. Your mother's glad that you're back. All of us here are glad."

"*Wado*, Uncle," said Carrier. "I too am glad to be back here, back home. There were a few times when I didn't think I'd make it."

"I knew that you would," said Dancing Rabbit, but he didn't bother to tell his nephew why he had been so confident. He didn't tell him about the surprise visit from Jisdu or about his own visits to Wasulu and old White Tobacco.

"Your leg is better," said Carrier, suddenly changing the subject.

"Yes," said Dancing Rabbit, "but it will never be good again. It will never be like it was before. I'm afraid that my traveling is over. You will have to do it all for us from now on, the traveling and the trading." Then he paused a moment before finishing his thought. "That is," he said, "if we continue with this trading at all."

"Why shouldn't we continue, Uncle?" said Carrier. "I went alone this time, and I made it back. You yourself just said that it was our most successful trip. I could do it again. Each time I should be better than the last, because I'll have more experience."

"That's true," said Dancing Rabbit. "You did do well, and of course experience makes you better. You're right about that, but I didn't know that I'd worry so much. I worried for your safety, of course, and I worried about the writing. What you've told me about the fighting with those invaders just makes me more certain that I should worry. It worked out all right this time, but it might not the next. If something happened to you, nephew, I don't know what I'd do about the writing. I have no one else."

A long pause followed. Both men stared at the ground in the silence of deep thought. At last Carrier spoke.

"Yes," he said. "I too had that thought about the writing. I knew that I had to get back home safely because of that."

"Well," said Dancing Rabbit, the relief obvious in his voice, "and now you have a wife, or you will have soon. Perhaps you should stay at home from here on. Perhaps you won't want to go away on long trips leaving her at home alone."

Carrier glanced in the direction of his mother's house, toward the location of what would be his wife's house. He recalled the feeling of the touch of Potmaker's skin, and he thought of long hours of lovemaking and long hours of idle conversation. He thought about teaching Potmaker the language of the Real People. He thought about the children they might have together, and, yes, he thought about the one she might have because of the *Ani-'squani*. He wondered if it would have hair on its face.

"You're right, Uncle," he said. "You're always right. I think I've had enough of traveling."

Glossary
Cherokee words, phrases, and names used in *The Way South*

Agıyosı   I'm hungry.

Ani-Chahta   Choctaw People or Choctaws. (*Ani* is a plural prefix.)

Ani-Cusa   Creek (or Muskogee) People or Creeks.

Ani-Kutani   the ancient priesthood among the Cherokees. Name cannot be translated. When they became too despotic, they were killed off in a popular uprising, the details of which are dealt with in Book II of *The Real People, The Dark Way*.

Ani-'squani   contraction of *Ani-Asquani*, Spanish People or Spaniards. The word is most likely a "Cherokeeized" version of the Spanish word *Español* (with the Cherokee plural prefix).

Ani-yunwi-ya   the Real People. The name that the Cherokees called themselves. "Cherokee" is not, apparently, a Cherokee word, but was applied to the Cherokees from outside. Cherokees today, however, do use the word "Cherokee" (*Tsalagi* when speaking Cherokee) and tend to translate *Ani-yunwi-ya* as "Indian."

Asquani   a Spaniard. See *Ani-'squani* above.

Atali-guli   Mountain Climber, a name for the ginseng plant. It is also called, more formally, *yunwi-usdi*, Little Man.

Do-na-da-go-huh-i   we shall see one another again.

Doya   beaver.

Gatayusti   a gambling game, played by rolling a stone disc and tossing a spear after it. More commonly known by the Creek name, Chunkey. In Cherokee mythology, the game was invented by Untsaiyi, the Gambler (see below).

Gogi   the Cherokee year is divided into two main parts: *Gogi*, the Time of the Snake, the warm time, from April to October, and *Gola*, the Time of the Eagle, the cold part, from the new moon in October until the new moon in April.

Guhwisida   dried or parched corn meal.

Iya-Iyusti   pumpkin-like (*iya*, pumpkin + *iyusti*, like).

Jisdu   rabbit.

Kalogwek'di   the locust tree or locust wood. (The apostrophe indicates a contraction, where a vowel sound has been dropped.)

Kanahena   a drink made from hominy corn, traditionally served to guests.

Kituwah   an ancient Cherokee word which cannot be translated. It was the name of a town, some say the Mother Town or one of the mother towns. Cherokees sometimes refer to themselves as *Ani-Kituwagi*, or Kituwah People. There is a traditional society among the Cherokees yet today called the Kituwah Society and there is a federally recognized tribal government in Oklahoma known as the United Keetoowah Band of Cherokees. The word is spelled variously: Kituwah, Keetoowah, Katuah.

Kutani   a priest. See *Ani-kutani* above.

Mi mi mi   onomatopoeia. A noise made by a rabbit.

Nihina   and you?

Nun-yunu-wi   "Dressed-in-Stone," sometimes translated as Stone-coat. A mythical Cherokee monster.

Osd' contraction of *osda*, good or well.

'Siyo contraction of *osiyo*, a greeting.

Su sa sai meaningless vocables in song, analogous to tra la la, or for the more modern listener, na na na.

Tohiju how are you?

Tsikilili a chickadee. It could be spelled *chikilili* or *jikilili*. The initial sound varies slightly in different dialects of the language.

Tsiyu yellow poplar (*chiyu* or *jiyu*).

Tsola gayunli ancient (sacred) tobacco (*tsola*, tobacco + *gayunli*, ancient). Or *chola* or *jola*.

Ujonati rattlesnake.

Uk'ten' contraction of *ukitena*, a mythical Cherokee monster, a giant snake with wings and antlers, very deadly.

Ulunsuti "transparent." A powerful divining crystal said to come from the forehead of an *uk'ten'* (see above).

Unahu heart. (The song of the titmouse sounds to the Cherokee ear like *unahu*.)

Untsaiyi sometimes contracted to *'tsaiyi*, onomatopoeia for the sound of something striking a sheet of metal. Analogous to "ping." Contemporarily it is translated as "brass." Also the name of a mythical Cherokee monster, the inventor of the *gatayusti* game. (See *gatayusti* above.)

Usquada buckeye.

U-tluh-da Spear-finger or Awl-finger. A mythical Cherokee monster.

Utsugi the titmouse.

Uwelanatsiga liver, I eat it.

Wado thank you.

Wanei hickory.

Wasulu a brown moth which hovers around tobacco plants.

Yansa buffalo.

Other Native American words (not Cherokee)

Alabama   a southeastern American Indian tribe speaking a Muskogean language, a member of the so-called Creek Confederacy.

Apalachee   a Muskogean-speaking southeastern people.

Calusa   a Muskogean-speaking people native to southern Florida.

Chiahas   a Muskogean-speaking southeastern people, member of the Creek Confederacy.

Chiloki   also spelled *Chilocki, Chalakee*. The word, probably of Muskogean origin and therefore used in the Mobilian trade language which was Choctaw-based, that was applied to the Real People by many of their neighboring tribes and eventually by the Europeans. It finally stuck in English as Cherokee and has since even been adopted by the Cherokees themselves in the Cherokee form, *Tsalagi* (*Chalagi* or *Jalagi*).

Hitchiti   a southeastern tribe, member of the Creek Confederacy.

Koasati   a southeastern people, member of the Creek Confederacy.

Muskogee   sometimes called Creek, the dominant tribe of the Creek Confederacy, also the designation (Muskogean) of a large American Indian language family.

Oconee   a southeastern tribe.

Okmulgee   a southeastern tribe, member of the Creek Confederacy.

Sawoklis   a southeastern tribe.

Timucua   a powerful tribe in northern Florida.

Tuskegees   a southeastern tribe.

Yuchi   a southeastern tribe, member of the Creek Confederacy.

ABOUT THE AUTHOR

Robert J. Conley is a Western writer and editor who specializes in Cherokee lore. He is the author of several previous Double D Westerns, including *The Way of the Priests*, *The Dark Way*, and *The White Path*. He has received Spur Awards from the Western Writers of America for his 1987 short story "Yellow Bird," and for his 1992 novel, *Nickajack*. He lives in Tahlequah, Oklahoma.

ABOUT THE ILLUSTRATOR

Painter/pipemaker Murv Jacob, a descendant of the Kentucky Cherokees, lives and works in Tahlequah, Oklahoma. His meticulously researched, brightly colored, intricate work centers on the traditional Southeastern cultures and has won numerous awards.